> **"We're married, Ethan.
> We want to make our commitment
> permanent." She took a short breath
> for courage. "We both know
> the only way to do that."**

Savannah faced him, her fingers immediately going to the top button of her blouse.

Ethan almost ran to stop her. "No," he said, clasping her fingers to remove them from the button.

"No?" she asked, wide-eyed, frightened and so incredibly beautiful in her innocence that he almost shook with gratitude.

"If we're going to do this we're going to do this right," he said.

Then he bent his head and kissed her....

Dear Reader,

Calling all royal watchers! This month, Silhouette Romance's Carolyn Zane kicks off our exciting new series, ROYALLY WED: THE MISSING HEIR, with the gem *Of Royal Blood*. Fans of last year's ROYALLY WED series will love this thrilling four-book adventure, filled with twists and turns—and of course, plenty of love and romance. Blue bloods and commoners alike will also enjoy Laurey Bright's newest addition to her VIRGIN BRIDES thematic series, *The Heiress Bride*, about a woman who agrees to marry to protect the empire that is rightfully hers.

This month is also filled with earth-shattering secrets! First, award-winning author Sharon De Vita serves up a whopper in her latest SADDLE FALLS title, *Anything for Her Family*. Natalie McMahon is much more than the twin boys' nanny—she's their mother! And in Karen Rose Smith's *A Husband in Her Eyes*, the heroine has her eyesight restored, only to have haunting visions of a man and child. Can she bring love and happiness back into their lives?

Everyone likes surprises, right? Well, in Susan Meier's *Married Right Away*, the heroine certainly gives her boss the shock of his life—she's having his baby! And Love Inspired author Cynthia Rutledge makes her Silhouette Romance debut with her modern-day Cinderella story, *Trish's Not-So-Little Secret*, about "Fatty Patty" who comes back to her hometown a beautiful swan—and a single mom with a jaw-dropping secret!

We hope this month that you feel like a princess and enjoy the royal treats we have for you from Silhouette Romance.

Happy reading!

Mary-Theresa Hussey

Mary-Theresa Hussey
Senior Editor

Please address questions and book requests to:
Silhouette Reader Service
U.S.: 3010 Walden Ave., P.O. Box 1325, Buffalo, NY 14269
Canadian: P.O. Box 609, Fort Erie, Ont. L2A 5X3

Married Right Away

SUSAN MEIER

SILHOUETTE *Romance*®

Published by Silhouette Books

America's Publisher of Contemporary Romance

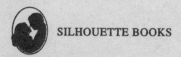 SILHOUETTE BOOKS

ISBN 0-373-19579-6

MARRIED RIGHT AWAY

Copyright © 2002 by Linda Susan Meier

This edition published by arrangement with Harlequin Books S.A.

® and TM are trademarks of Harlequin Books S.A., used under license. Trademarks indicated with ® are registered in the United States Patent and Trademark Office, the Canadian Trade Marks Office and in other countries.

Visit Silhouette at www.eHarlequin.com

Printed in U.S.A.

Books by Susan Meier

Silhouette Romance

Stand-in Mom #1022
Temporarily Hers #1109
Wife in Training #1184
Merry Christmas, Daddy #1192
In Care of the Sheriff #1283
Guess What? We're Married! #1338
Husband from 9 to 5 #1354
The Rancher and the Heiress #1374
†*The Baby Bequest* #1420
†*Bringing up Babies* #1427
†*Oh, Babies!* #1433
His Expectant Neighbor #1468
Hunter's Vow #1487
Cinderella and the CEO #1498
Marrying Money #1519
The Boss's Urgent Proposal #1566
Married Right Away #1579

Silhouette Desire

Take the Risk #567

*Texas Family Ties
†Brewster Baby Boom

SUSAN MEIER

is one of eleven children, and though she has yet to write a book about a big family, many of her books explore the dynamics of "unusual" family situations like large work "families," bosses who behave like overprotective fathers, or "sister" bonds created between friends. Because she has more than twenty nieces and nephews, children are also always popping up in her stories. Many of the funny scenes in her books are based upon experiences raising her own children or interacting with her nieces and nephews.

She was born and raised in western Pennsylvania and continues to live in Pennsylvania.

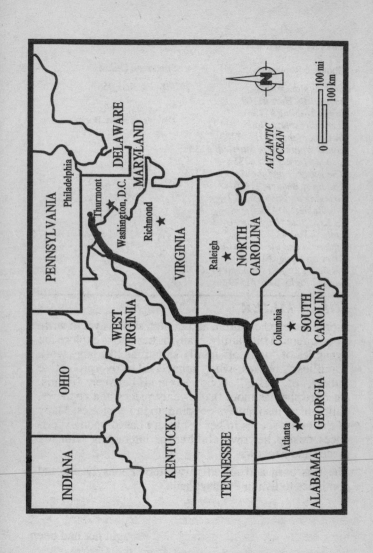

Chapter One

When Savannah Groggin opened the door of her Thurmont, Maryland, bed-and-breakfast to Ethan McKenzie, she wasn't surprised to see her former boss, the in-house counsel for an Atlanta-based company where she had worked as a paralegal.

"Savannah, I'm so sorry," Ethan said, as he entered her foyer. His short black hair was combed in the usual neat style she remembered from two years before. His brown eyes were serious, concerned. But wearing blue jeans and a T-shirt and not dressed in a suit, he looked much younger than she remembered. Also, the casual clothes made him seem more approachable than he had been when she worked for him, which was the first and only good thing she had noticed all day.

"*You're* sorry?" Savannah said, looking at the floor because she couldn't meet his eyes. In just twelve short hours, all the joy her pregnancy had brought her had been lost. Not only had she learned from the Georgia State Police that the sperm donation used to create the baby she carried belonged to her ex-boss, but also that her brother was a fugitive from justice. She bit her bottom lip to keep it from trembling, then said, "My brother and I are the ones who should be sorry."

"I know you didn't have anything to do with this," he said urgently. "From the way this thing was set up, the police deduced you're innocent. But even if they hadn't told me you weren't an accomplice, I worked with you long enough to realize, well, that you hadn't known—"

"That my brother falsified records at the clinic where he worked and stole your sperm?"

Ethan grimaced at her frankness, then nodded. "Yes."

Confused and tired from a long, difficult day, Savannah rubbed her hands along the small of her back. "Since we have a lot to talk about, could we sit in the living room?"

Ethan's expression became distressed and his gaze fell to her stomach, which wasn't yet huge with child, but was obviously swollen.

Suddenly, it hit her full force.

The baby in her belly belonged to both of them.

He cleared his throat. "Savannah, I'm sorry. I should have thought of that," he said as he took her hand and led her into her quiet living room. Furnished with aging blue French provincial furniture trimmed in walnut, with thick navy velour drapes in front of white lace sheers, the room was dark and quiet.

Savannah turned on a lamp, shedding some much-needed light into the room, and sat on the sofa.

Ethan sat beside her and took her hand again. "Is there anything I can get you?"

"No. I'm fine." Part of her almost wished he wouldn't be so nice because it made her feel incredibly guilty. The other part was glad he was handling this better than she was. It was hard enough to come to terms with the fact that her brother had forged someone's name, falsified records and stolen property all because she was concerned about getting a good father for the in vitro fertilization. It was almost too much to bear that Barry felt the only way he could fulfill his promise to her was to cheat a man she knew and respected.

Tightening his hold on her hand, Ethan said, "Savannah, though your brother had no right to do what he did, I also have to take some responsibility. I should have destroyed that sample two years ago when my wife and I divorced."

"It's very nice of you to say that," Savannah said. "But you entrusted your property to a reputable clinic. You shouldn't have had to worry that someone would steal it."

"True. But I didn't do what I was supposed to do, so I'm accountable, too," Ethan said, sounding logical yet kind.

Immediately Savannah's instincts went on red alert. She remembered that as an attorney this man was sharp and intelligent. There was only one reason he would take responsibility. He wanted it. And if he wanted responsibility that meant he wanted the baby.

In all the confusion about her brother, her fear of being thought of as an accomplice and her hours of being questioned by the police, Savannah hadn't forgotten the real issue wasn't the crime, but the baby. A man didn't cryogenically preserve his sperm unless he wanted to assure he had a child someday. Though she probably wasn't the mother he would have chosen, and this might not be the time he would have preferred, the deed was done. He had his child on the way. And he would get it.

Ethan might genuinely believe Savannah hadn't been in on the scheme, but her brother's misdeeds would cast a shadow of doubt on her credibility in court. Plus, Ethan was a wealthy man from a prominent, well-respected family. His father had been a senator forever. His mother had served on a president's cabinet. Her baby, the baby she had been carrying for five months, the child she wanted more than her next breath of air, was as good as lost to her.

Desperately trying not to cry, she nervously fingered the long strawberry blond curls that fell across her shoulders to her bosom. "You want custody of the baby, don't you?"

"Custody is one of the things we need to talk about."

"Okay," Savannah said, nearly paralyzed with fear. Tears threatened beneath her eyelids. She had gone through the tests, the processes, the first five months of pregnancy filled with so much joy that she could barely contain it. She wasn't ready to let her unborn baby slip through her fingers. Not yet. "What are the other things you want to talk about?"

For several seconds, Ethan said nothing, then finally, quietly, he said, "I've been told my father's friend, Sam Ringer, has decided to run for president of the United States and my father is his vice presidential choice. But Sam isn't waiting around for his party's convention to announce it. He's announcing it in the fall so he can use my father's pull to help him win the primaries and assure he gets the nomination."

"Oh, my God," Savannah said, feeling all the blood drain from her face, as the situation continued to worsen. Her baby had been created without permission. Her brother was a fugitive. The McKenzies were rich and powerful and would probably take her to court to get this child. And her custody battle with the son of a vice presidential candidate would probably start around the same time as the first primary, so every unhappy fact of her life would be fodder for the national news.

The picture of it flashed in her mind. She could see microphones and cameras shoved in her face, and vans with satellite dishes parked in her yard.

She shook her head in dismay. "This is going to be a circus."

Ethan shifted on his seat. "Not really. I mean, it doesn't have to be," he said softly. Still holding her hand, he lightly tugged on her fingers and forced her to look at him. "Savannah, the only thing that makes this news is that your brother falsified records and you were impregnated without my knowledge. But if everybody thought you were pregnant because we were lovers, it wouldn't be a big deal."

Remembering again how cunning this man could be, a chill snaked through her. "So you want me to pretend we've been dating?"

He shook his head and said, "No, I want you to marry me."

Savannah's heart felt like it stopped beating. She laid her free hand on her chest. "Marry you?" she whispered.

"If you don't marry me, and this story leaks to the press as it is, your brother will be the most popular, most sought-after fugitive in the world if only by the tabloids, and my father will be answering more questions about this baby than about real campaign issues. This story could overshadow every point he and Senator Ringer try to make and render their campaign irrelevant.

"But if you marry me," Ethan continued, "I won't press charges against your brother. He won't be a wanted man anymore and our pregnancy and wedding will be a blip in the human interest pages of a few newspapers. Nothing more.''

''I see,'' Savannah said, though she could hardly believe what she was hearing. Yesterday she was the simple, humble owner of a bed-and-breakfast that she had inherited when her parents were killed. Today she was receiving a proposal of marriage from a man considered one of the most eligible bachelors in the nation—because she was pregnant with his child and that child had been created in an unorthodox way, a way that involved forgery and theft.

''Before you agree,'' Ethan said, again catching her gaze. ''I have to tell you that if this is going to work we'll also have to make everyone believe we're a love match. That doesn't mean that I'm going to fawn all over you, or that I'll expect you to be my wife for real and forever. But it does mean that we'll have to pretend to be in love for the general public, including my parents, and that you'll need to move to Atlanta with me until after the baby is born. We'll wait a month or two after that to make everything seem legitimate then we'll quietly divorce.''

Savannah swallowed hard. ''I need to move to Atlanta?''

''Yes. It's where I live. It's where you lived until two years ago. We worked together. It won't be a stretch for people to believe we had a relationship.''

Overwhelmed with facts and possibilities, most of them bad, Savannah drew a long breath. ''If I marry you, does this mean you won't fight me for custody?''

''If you marry me I won't fight you for custody, but visitation is an entirely different thing. I don't want to be a weekend dad. I will be a big part of this child's life.''

Well, the cards were on the table, Savannah thought,

not entirely pleased, but at least relieved that Ethan wouldn't take away her basic right as a mother. She knew she could probably use the marriage as further leverage to push him into some kind of visitation agreement right now, but she also recognized that she had more immediate concerns.

She couldn't handle a cub reporter on a good day. Even though leaving her bed-and-breakfast posed an enormous problem for her, if only because she had bookings, getting her friends to take over for a few months was easier than defending her brother, herself and her baby in the court of public opinion.

She also had to take a share of the responsibility for Barry's forgery and theft because she had made him promise she would get a good father for her baby. She had to take some responsibility for that, too.

Ethan again squeezed her fingers gently. "Savannah, I didn't expect you to answer today. But I will need an answer first thing tomorrow."

Glad to have a reprieve to think this through, Savannah tried to smile, but failed miserably. "Okay."

"Just remember that the longer you take to decide the less possible this scheme becomes," he said quietly. He studied her, then rubbed his thumb across her knuckles. "Today, the clinic and a handful of police know. By tomorrow night, you can add a hundred people to that list. This time next week, you can add millions. But with the right word from me, I can have that police report filed away or destroyed as if it never existed."

"What about the people at the sperm bank?"

Ethan smiled. "Since I could sue the clinic into bankruptcy for this, once I tell the owner I'm not pressing charges, a smart man would shove the paperwork so far back in the corner of his filing cabinet that it would never again see the light of day. Even if one of the employees sold the story to a tabloid, with that paperwork 'lost' there would be nothing to back it up and we could easily deny it.

"But if we let another twenty-four hours go by," Ethan continued, "then this window of opportunity is gone because too many people will know the truth. You need to agree before seven tomorrow morning or all bets are off."

Savannah nodded.

"Okay. I'm going to let you alone now to think about this because I can tell by looking at you that you've had enough excitement for one day."

His voice softened marginally and Savannah recognized that though he was pushing her into making a huge decision, he was doing it gently, like a man taking care of her. Only then did it fully register that he was still sitting beside her, holding her hand. And only then did the knowledge that she was pregnant with *his* child completely sink in. Her body flushed as the heat of embarrassment spiraled through her. Though they hadn't been physically "intimate" with each other, they were none the less sharing the most intimate experience any two people could share. Together they had created a child, a child who was growing inside her.

Savannah felt strange and awkward and suddenly faint.

Grateful that he was leaving, she cautiously slid her hand from his and took a slow breath before she said, "You're right. I've had so much news in the past twelve hours that I need time to digest at least some of it before I can make this decision."

"You rest then," he said, rising. "And I'll be back early tomorrow morning."

Savannah nodded and rose from the sofa, too. As she

did she noticed the way the lamplight glistened off Ethan's shiny black hair. Though she didn't want to be making these kinds of observations, she realized that her child could look exactly like him. He or she might have Ethan's eyes and Ethan's hair. Their baby could have his brains and his talent, or, better yet, their baby could really be somebody important like Ethan's father....

Reminded of the prominence of Ethan's family, the queasy feeling in her stomach turned into full-fledged nausea. She had just been asked to marry the son of a man who might become the next vice president of the United States. Worse, he was one of the most eligible bachelors in the world because he wasn't merely rich, he was gorgeous. Absolutely gorgeous. She'd noticed before, of course. She would have been blind not to, but working with him and being married to him were two different things.

"We will be getting divorced, right?"

"As soon as reasonably possible after the baby's born," Ethan agreed, walking to the door. "But that gives us time to talk about visitation."

Ethan smiled at her and Savannah returned his smile, but Ethan didn't for one second believe she was okay with all this. Which suited him just fine because he wasn't a hundred percent sure he was okay with it, either. In fact, having her wary rather than excited at the prospect of becoming his wife was actually a point in her favor. He meant it when he said he didn't think she had any knowledge of this scheme to use his sperm, but now that the baby had been created, he had to take steps to ensure she didn't get any crazy ideas. Like blackmail. The shy, sweet paralegal he worked with two years ago would never think to use his child as a ploy to get money but he wasn't so sure about the new Savannah he had found here this evening.

She didn't even look like the woman he remembered. Instead of having short unruly red hair, she now had long tresses that cascaded all around her so that the riot of curls was flattering, not disheveled. Though her pregnancy concealed it, she must have lost some weight because her face was thinner...prettier. She wasn't wearing an ounce of makeup, yet she looked beautiful in a way she never had when she worked at Hilton-Cooper-Martin Foods. The past two years had matured her into an absolutely stunning woman.

A stunning woman swollen with *his* child, Ethan thought, then swallowed hard. She wasn't merely a beautiful woman to whom he would be attracted if circumstances were different, she was somebody he had worked with, a wonderfully innocent woman he had liked and respected, and the baby she carried was his. He wanted to hug her. He wanted to take care of her. He wanted to forget that this situation had repercussions and allow himself to tumble headfirst into the magic of becoming a parent. He wanted to bask in the knowledge that finally—after thirty-five years—he was about to become a father!

But he couldn't. He knew he couldn't. He wasn't entirely sure how this situation was going to play out. So he had to be ready for whenever Savannah decided to make her move....

Still he allowed himself one tiny father-to-be indulgence and asked, "Are you okay to be alone tonight?"

"I'm fine," Savannah said. "I just need to get accustomed to all this."

"Yeah, me, too," Ethan agreed, because he was sure that once his own astonishment and excitement abated, he wouldn't have to worry about being attracted to her or overwhelmed with the joy of becoming a father. His common sense and logic would return and he would be just fine.

But when he again caught her gaze, he saw sadness in her eyes and suddenly recognized that while he was fighting the desire to rejoice over getting a child she was being forced to adjust to having to share her child. From the pain in her eyes it was a devastating blow.

Again he remembered her as she was when she worked with him. Shy. Sweet. Vulnerable. Guilt tightened his chest and made him draw a deep breath.

"I know this has been an awful day for you. I don't feel right leaving you by yourself."

"I'm not going to be by myself. I have friends coming over in a few minutes," she said, backing away from him. "Since I got pregnant, we've made Friday night our poker night."

"Poker?"

The question in his voice must have amused her, because she smiled. "What? You think women don't like to gamble a little or get together for a weekly gossip session?"

He wished she hadn't told him she liked to gamble, but in some ways he was glad she had because it brought him back to earth with a hard thump. He didn't know how much she had changed in the past two years. She might not have had any part in stealing his property, but now that she knew he was the father of her baby it wasn't a stretch to realize she would soon see she could make this work in her favor.

Before Ethan had a chance to say anything, there was a quick knock at the door. Her guests didn't wait for an invitation to enter, and Ethan had to jump out of the way as the women he assumed were her poker pals entered around him. Redheaded twins, a blonde and a brunette made up the quartet. Each of the women was in her early twenties. All wore simple jeans and colorful T-shirts.

"Hi, Savannah!"

"Hi." She paused, glanced at Ethan and drew a quick breath. "This is Ethan McKenzie. Ethan, these are my friends, Andi, Mandi, Becki and Lindsay."

Ethan said, "How do you do?"

"How do you do…?"

Four pair of eyes eagerly assessing him might have cowed another man, but Ethan held their gazes steadily, making his own quick assessment of things. Just from the cornered expression on the face of the brunette, Ethan knew her poker buddies weren't simply here for a night of playing cards. He would bet his last dime they came here every Friday night more to check up on Savannah than to gamble and they would take care of her. The smartest thing for him to do would be to get the hell out of here and regroup before he said or did something that he regretted, if only out of compassion for the woman carrying his child.

His child.

He almost couldn't believe he was about to have a baby. The knowledge overwhelmed him. Took his breath. Which was exactly why he had to be careful. The last time he let an emotion control him, it cost him much more than he could afford to risk.

He looked at Savannah and forced himself to see her objectively, honestly and through the filter of unhappy possibilities. "We'll talk tomorrow."

She nodded. "Okay."

The second he was out the door, Savannah turned to her four friends. Protectively placing her palm on her stomach, she said, "I'm in big trouble."

"What?" Becki, one of the twins, groaned. "Please don't tell me that good-looking guy is suing you or something."

"Or something," Savannah said, leading her friends into the living room, where they sat on the sofa and round-backed chairs, tucking their feet beneath them and getting comfortable, though they continued to stare at Savannah with rapt attention.

"He's the father of this baby," Savannah said, then looked from blond-haired, blue-eyed Lindsay, to the red-haired twins Mandi and Becki, to dark-haired, dark-eyed Andi. "I didn't know it. He didn't know it. But *Barry* did. Ethan had sperm cryogenically frozen for some reason when he was married. Apparently, my fear about getting a good father for the baby led Barry to search the banks of people who had sperm stored but weren't donors. When he found Ethan's name he knew we had our father because we knew Ethan to be a good man since I had worked with him. So Barry forged Ethan's signature to get his sample mainstreamed into the donor banks to be used for *my* pregnancy."

"Oh, boy," Mandi said slowly, her blue eyes widening with each word.

"Yeah, oh, boy."

"So, is this guy pressing charges?" Lindsay demanded.

Savannah licked her lips. "Not if I marry him."

"You're kidding!" Becki gasped, flopping back on her chair as if flabbergasted.

"It gets worse. His father is…"

"Parker McKenzie," Andi said. A reporter who was part of a team that covered the Washington beat for several newspapers, Andi knew everybody on Capitol Hill. She had facts at her disposal that the general public wouldn't have. She also knew backgrounds that frequently got forgotten. "He's a senator who had to live down the pasts of a starlet mother and drug-using pro-football player father. His son's sperm theft would be the final embarrassment of his career. But his son's marriage, even a hasty marriage, would go virtually unnoticed."

"That's approximately what Ethan said," Savannah confirmed.

"He's right," Andi said, combing her fingers through the mop of thick, blunt cut sable hair that fell to her shoulders. "A marriage would make this 'problem' a nonissue."

"So you think I should marry him?"

"I don't know what *you* should do—" Andi began.

"Marrying him virtually guarantees legal standing in a custody suit," Mandi interrupted.

"He doesn't need to marry her to get legal standing," Lindsay said, as all eyes turned to the law student. "He has legal standing. He is the baby's father. Actually, it's probably more documented than if you had gotten pregnant because you were lovers. He doesn't even need DNA tests. He has papers that prove his sperm created your baby."

All eyes then turned to Savannah. "Does he have papers?" Becki asked.

"The Georgia State Police told me Barry forged Ethan's signature to mainstream his sperm for use by the clinic. So, that's one paper. They also had search warrants that let them roam the entire bed-and-breakfast looking for clues of where Barry might be. Since police don't get search warrants from judges without a good reason, I'm assuming it's all documented somewhere and that's why Barry went into hiding."

Becki caught Savannah's gaze. "Do you know where Barry is?"

Savannah shook her head. "No. All I know is he called me and told me that he was leaving for a new job in Canada. Though he avoided telling me where the job was, I knew something was wrong. Then eight hours after he called, the police arrived and told me that when the clinic was auditing their procedures, they randomly chose my pregnancy to follow to make sure everything had been done properly. Apparently, Barry only got away because he saw what case they were going to audit and he left before they began pulling files. No one noticed he was gone until after they called Ethan. Because he had not originally been a sperm donor, they had to confirm he had reclassified his sample. Ethan, of course, had not. When they started putting two and two together with my pregnancy, Ethan's reclassified sperm and Barry's absence, it was already too late."

"He does look guilty," Becki said sadly.

"Yeah, he does," Savannah agreed. "The ironic thing is that I don't even know where to find him to tell him Ethan is dropping the charges if I marry him."

"And just like that Barry can come home?" Mandi said skeptically. "No punishment, no problems."

"He didn't really do anything wrong," Savannah insisted. "I'm the one who said I couldn't do this without a guarantee that I would get a good father. He promised me a good father. He delivered."

"Yeah, he delivered, all right," Becki said. "He could have delivered you to a jail cell."

"That's not what he intended."

"Savannah, you've got to quit defending that kid," Mandi said.

But Lindsay stopped her with a look. "Barry is Savannah's brother," she quietly reminded Mandi, but Savannah knew what she was really saying.

"He's my only family," she said, not needing to remind everybody of past tragedies. "Besides if I don't marry Ethan, he could sue for custody. And he'll win because I can't fight the McKenzie money."

"Oh, Savannah," Andi said, jumping from her chair to rush over and hug Savannah. "I don't think you need to worry about him suing for custody. These people can't afford bad press. Even if you don't marry him, I don't think he's going to try to take this baby away from you."

"You think the baby's safe?"

"I think that if you stand your ground, the McKenzies will settle for whatever you are willing to give them to keep this out of the papers."

"I agree," Lindsay said, obviously thinking this through from a legal perspective. "Fathers have more rights than they used to, but if the McKenzies try for custody it will end up as a lawsuit. And if what you're saying is true, Ethan McKenzie can't afford an ugly lawsuit any more than he can afford for this story to leak. You've got some leverage here, too. If nothing else, you can expose the truth."

"Except you don't have the papers that prove any of it, do you?" Becki asked.

Savannah shook her head. "No."

"Then get them," Lindsay said. "Don't wait until the evidence is mysteriously lost or destroyed. Call tomorrow. Because whether you marry him or not, the papers that prove you used in vitro fertilization are your best bet for making sure Ethan sticks to any deal you guys make.''

''You mean I'm going to have to resort to blackmail?''

''It's not blackmail,'' Andi said, placing her hand on top of Savannah's in a gesture of support. ''Just insurance.''

''Yeah, insurance,'' Becki said, putting her hand on top of Andi's in a show of solidarity.

Though Savannah smiled and nodded, she wasn't convinced this was the right thing to do. She was pregnant because of a forgery. She was getting married to cover up a theft. And she would be getting the papers to prove it all.

She couldn't help but think that if the original two wrongs didn't make a right, getting the papers that proved them would do nothing but cause more trouble. Still, she saw what her friends were getting at.

''I'll call tomorrow.''

''Early,'' Mandi insisted.

She nodded and tried to smile, but couldn't. In spite of the fact that it seemed like the right thing to do, she had a really bad feeling about this. Particularly since Ethan said he could have the paperwork shoved to a back corner of a filing cabinet by seven o'clock tomorrow morning. *Saturday* morning. They were about to enter a weekend where offices would be closed and police would be busier than normal. It was no wonder Ethan was so confident he could quash this story. By Monday morning the paperwork would be gone and everyone's memory would be dulled by rapes and murders and drug busts.

''I think I'll call Barry's boss at home. Tonight.''

Chapter Two

The next morning, when Savannah opened her door to Ethan McKenzie, birds chirped in the trees in the front yard of her yellow Victorian home. The flowers lining her sidewalk and in the beds surrounding the wide gray porch seemed to be yawning and stretching in anticipation of the new June day. The sun was in the final stages of rising, leaving a band of pale reds and muted blues along the charcoal horizon, but there was sufficient light that Savannah noticed the strain in Ethan's face, the tautness of his muscles, the caution in his approach.

"Good morning, Savannah."

"Good morning, Ethan," she said, motioning for him to enter.

She didn't blame him for being tense. A great deal was at stake in this bargain. Not just his father's career and her brother's future, but also the future of their baby. Fortunately for her, she had spoken with Barry's boss and with her own attorney in Thurmont, so she also wasn't worried about custody anymore. Within a few days, she would hold the trump card in her hands. Though the proof of how their child was created had originally hurt her, it would now protect her. Even if she didn't make any deal with Ethan, those papers were her insurance that he wouldn't take away her baby.

Knowing her child was safe, she now had to do whatever she could to free Barry and protect Ethan's father.

"I've decided getting married solves both of our problems," she said immediately, if only because Ethan's expression indicated he had worried about her answer. "I appreciate that you didn't push me last night. But even after a few hours to think about the situation, I couldn't come up with a better solution. So I'm in."

To her amazement, he seemed to sag with relief. "And today we can finalize everything?"

"I think so," she said, leading him into her kitchen. She wouldn't tell him that after a short discussion with the clinic director about the right of an accused to see any evidence presented against him, he had agreed that she and Barry should be allowed access to the records once they secured legal authorization. She also wouldn't disclose that she had contacted her attorney, Wallace Jeffries, who was in the process of drawing up legal documents. She was sure that behind the scenes Ethan was doing his level best to protect himself, too. He would be crazy if he wasn't. And he would be naive to think she would go into this without precautions of her own. There was no need to discuss it. No need to threaten him. No need to tip her hand. Besides, if Ethan stuck to whatever bargain they made, she would never even use the information.

She led Ethan through the swinging door into her kitchen. Delicious aromas from freshly baked cinnamon rolls and coffee greeted them.

"Would you like something? Coffee? Maybe a cinnamon roll?"

Savannah watched Ethan glance at the syrupy rolls sitting on a plate in the center of her round table. "Did you just bake those?"

She grinned. "This morning."

"Oh, God, please," he said with a groan of pleasure. "Coffee and one of those rolls sounds like heaven."

"Coming right up," she said and gathered a plate, cup, saucer and appropriate silverware for her guest. For the first time since his arrival at her house the night before, she heard a tone of normalcy sneaking into their conversation and she desperately wanted to keep it. They didn't merely need to be comfortable with each other to negotiate visitation fairly. They also needed to relax because they would be living together until after the baby was born. Somehow, they had to break through the awkwardness between them once and for all to make their lives bearable until they divorced.

Trying to lighten the mood, she said, "Marrying me is going to have some hidden advantages. I bake like no one you know."

"So it seems," he agreed, but his voice was oddly quiet. Almost reverent.

She turned and caught him staring at her stomach and recognition of what he was thinking sent a ripple of unease through her and breathed new life into the tension she had hoped was dying. Though they had both had less than twenty-four hours to acclimate to the fact that they were having a baby together, she had had five months to adapt to being pregnant. For him, all of this was still new and until he got accustomed to her pregnancy he would not be comfortable with her.

She licked her dry lips. "Pretty amazing isn't it?"

His gaze didn't move from her tummy. "Fascinating."

"As my stomach grows, I realize the baby is getting bigger, becoming more developed, and it just sort of blows me away."

"I can understand that," Ethan whispered.

Savannah took a long breath and set the plate and utensils on the countertop. He sounded like an outsider looking in, and she realized that was the problem. As the baby's father, he had as much right to be part of this experience as she had. Once he got those rights, once this pregnancy became as much his as it was hers, the awkwardness would vanish.

"Would you like to touch?" she softly offered.

Though he wore jeans and a simple shirt, he straightened in his chair as if he were wearing a three-piece suit and carrying a briefcase. "No. No. That's not necessary. I'm sorry, Savannah. I don't mean to be staring."

She took a few steps closer to the table. "Ethan, this is your baby, too."

His gaze fell to her stomach again. "I know."

"And it's good for you to want to be a part of things."

He raised his dark brown eyes until they met hers. "You think?"

"Sure," she cheerfully agreed, though her heart was beating a million miles a second because they were face-to-face with the intimacy that was actually the catalyst of their nervousness. When they worked together they hadn't even been friends, just acquaintances. They never expected to be intimate, and didn't want to be intimate, but they now couldn't avoid it. So it was better to hit it head-on, because once they faced this, there would be nothing to be tense about anymore.

She lifted the loose T-shirt she wore over maternity

jeans, exposing the smooth porcelain mound containing their baby.

But Ethan didn't move. It hardly seemed as if he were breathing.

Savannah reached down and took his hand and placed it on her warm stomach. The baby picked that precise second to move. Slowly, gently, the tiny body shifted, causing a soft ripple across her tummy. Not something you could see, only something you could feel. Ethan's gaze shot to hers.

"That's him?"

Savannah inclined her head and suppressed a smile. "Or her."

The baby moved again and Ethan grinned. "Or her," he agreed, then laughed out loud. "My God, I can't believe it. I'm going to have a baby," he said, his voice dripping with awe.

"Technically *I'm* going to have the baby," she said, stepping away because she was experiencing weird sensations, none of which had anything to do with her pregnancy. Staring into Ethan's affection-filled brown eyes, she had felt as if she were bathed in warmth. Her skin felt silky and tingly at the same time, and she wanted nothing more than to lose herself in the moment.

Which wasn't just wrong, it was dangerous. She didn't really know Ethan's full intentions about their child, but she did know he wasn't marrying her because he loved her. With all the hormones floating around in her system and the loneliness that often consumed her, it would be very easy for her to misinterpret his affection for the baby as affection for her. She had to keep up her guard. Not lose her head. Not do something foolish.

She lowered her top to cover her tummy and turned to the counter again to retrieve the dishes and utensils. Quietly, she took them to the table. When she turned again to get the coffeepot, Ethan stopped her with a hand on her forearm.

Again, the silky feeling floated through her.

"You don't have to wait on me. I can get my own coffee. You sit."

Their gazes locked and, once again, Savannah felt she could get lost in his eyes. Almost black and warm with emotion, they held her as surely as the grip of a hand. She reminded herself that their baby inspired the tenderness she saw in Ethan's eyes. She told herself it had nothing to do with her, but that didn't stop the flood of recognition that flowed through her. Whether it was wise or not, at this precise moment she wasn't thinking about the baby. She was thinking about how attractive *he* was. How awful his divorce had been. How genuinely kind he had been to her when her parents died. What she was experiencing was an appreciation for him as a man.

Tall and lean, he had the structure and solidness of someone upon whom she could depend, and his behavior backed that up. He hadn't demanded she marry him. He hadn't waved his family's money or position to threaten her. He had asked her to marry him and given her time to think it through because he was intelligent, responsible and fair. For Savannah that was every bit as sexy as his compelling dark eyes, beautiful black hair and the cute little cleft in his chin.

Perhaps if the situation were different, if she had met him on the street and didn't have any prior association with him, she might want to flirt with him, wishing he would ask her out, wondering what it would be like to be his wife. Instead, they did have a connection, she didn't dare flirt with him. And in a few days or weeks, whatever timeline they decided this morning, she would be his wife.

The thought shot a shiver through her and she backed away from the table. If she didn't watch herself, she could end up in big trouble here. She could easily fall in love with this guy and end up completely brokenhearted.

When Savannah stepped away from the table, Ethan rose to get his coffee from the pot on the counter. Lifting the container, he noticed his hand was shaking and he knew why. When he put his palm on her abdomen, he felt a zing that had nothing to do with the baby he was touching and everything to do with Savannah. Logically he knew that was because he hadn't really touched a baby. He had touched *her.* He had stroked the soft skin of her tummy. And he felt a hundred emotions he had no right to feel. Appreciation. Wonder. Awe. And affection. He could put his genuine affection for Savannah down to having worked with her for two years, and he did, but he wasn't so foolish as to not realize that with very little help his feelings for this woman could explode.

And that would be trouble.

He had exonerated her, and he wasn't pressing charges against her brother. In return, she was helping him cover the problem so that the press didn't hurt his father. They were working together amicably, but that didn't mean he should relax with her. He didn't really know that she wouldn't take advantage of this situation to extort money. But even if she was sufficiently cleared of that, he couldn't afford to get emotionally involved with another woman.

Unfortunately, if he got any more appreciative of Savannah, he wouldn't merely be involved, he would be smitten. Then he would give her anything she wanted when they divorced, and that took him back to his bottom-line suspicion. Savannah might not have helped her brother cook up the scheme to get a part of the McKenzie money, but now that she had her foot in the door there was no telling what she could demand. Though he didn't believe Savannah was greedy, he couldn't completely leave himself and his family unprotected, either. Which meant he couldn't act upon any feelings he had for Savannah beyond what was appropriate.

"So, when do you want to get married?" he asked, taking his coffee to the table.

She shrugged. "I need two weeks to help my friends create a schedule and train them so they can run the bed-and-breakfast for the months I'm gone. Plus, we'll need time to get a license and do whatever else is required to get married in Maryland."

"That makes sense. How about the Saturday after next, then?"

She nodded. "The Saturday after next," she said, playing with her silverware as Ethan helped himself to one of her delicious-looking cinnamon rolls, if only to give her a few seconds to acclimate. He knew her entire life was being turned upside down, but there was no help for it. Getting married was the only way to protect his father.

"So...have you told your parents?"

He glanced at her. "I'm not going to."

She gasped. "You're not?"

"Not on your life. I discussed this with Hilton last night," he said, referring to Hilton Martin, family friend of the McKenzies, owner of Hilton-Cooper-Martin Foods and a man Ethan knew Savannah very much liked and respected. "And he agrees that there is no reason for my parents to know. Actually, their not knowing will help keep the scenario safe for them. Because they don't know the truth, they won't ever be lying to the press."

"That makes sense," Savannah agreed quietly.

"Yes, it does. The fewer people who know, the better," he began, but he suddenly realized something he should have thought of immediately and he almost groaned. "Savannah, did you tell anyone how you got pregnant?"

Obviously realizing why he had asked, Savannah grimaced, "This isn't something you share with the general public, so I only told the four women you met last night and Olivia Brady."

"Olivia Brady? From Hilton-Cooper-Martin Foods?" Ethan said, stiffening with fear that his perfect plan had a big hole in it.

"I didn't actually tell her everything when I had lunch with her in March. I tried, but she thought I was only considering getting pregnant and she never let me finish the story."

Ethan relaxed. "So, that's good, then. At the very least it's manageable. We can say we bumped into each other while you were in Atlanta, realized we were head over heels in love and keep the story as pure as the driven snow."

"I wouldn't call this story as pure as the driven snow," Savannah said, again playing with her silverware. "It's a lie."

"Yes, but it's a necessary lie," Ethan insisted. "What about your friends?"

"What about my friends?"

"What did you tell them?"

For this she looked him right in the eye. "I told them exactly what you told Hilton Martin."

Understanding the comparison she had deliberately

made, Ethan sucked in his breath. He couldn't criticize her for telling her friends because he had confided in Hilton. "Do you trust them?"

Savannah gaped at him. "Of course, I trust them! I trust them enough that they'll be running my business for six months."

"This is different...."

"I don't see how. Besides, even if I hadn't wanted to talk with them about this last night to get my bearings, I would have had to tell them something to give them a reason for why I was marrying somebody they didn't know and pulling up stakes. But only for six months. Not forever. Which immediately would alert them that something was wrong. There was no way I could have lied to them."

"Right. You're right. And I'm sorry."

"Okay."

Looking at Savannah's angry face, Ethan suddenly felt like the villain. And he wasn't. Her brother was. He wouldn't be coercing her into marriage if it weren't for her brother.

Nonetheless, guilt swamped him because he was asking a great deal of this woman. Then concern for her safety struck him next. What the hell was he doing upsetting the mother of his child? But continued fear about her friends hit him last and when that wave came it was a tsunami because it was a deal breaker. He wasn't afraid one of them had already leaked her secret. Up to now the details of her pregnancy were highly personal for Savannah, a secret easily kept among friends. But now that the information had real value in the tabloid marketplace, Ethan knew any one of those four women could decide to sell this story. Which would make getting married

pointless. If even *one* of them wasn't as trustworthy as
Savannah believed, this plan was dead in the water.

Still, not wanting to upset her with any more questions
about her friends, and knowing she would be biased anyway, Ethan decided he wouldn't say another word, but
would check out her friends on his own.

"Why don't you go change while I call my attorney
to see what we have to do to get married in Maryland."

"We have to see an attorney for that?"

"Well, we're also going to need to have a prenup
drawn up. Nothing extravagant, just one that says what's
mine is mine and what's yours is yours."

"Okay," she said, then licked her lips.

Ethan's gaze was drawn to her mouth. He noticed her
lips were lush and pink. Full. Very kissable. If he hadn't
already reminded himself of all the reasons he couldn't
encourage his attraction to her, he would have been very
tempted to at least wonder what it would be like to kiss
her. But he wasn't. He couldn't take the risk.

"Okay. We'll hash out the details at Gerry Smith's
office," he said. "You go ahead and get changed."

He watched her walk out of the kitchen, and after she
was gone, he combed his fingers through his hair in frus-
tration. It bugged the hell out of him that she made him
feel guilty for pushing her into this scheme when she
could be planning to turn around and blackmail him. Before he could enter into this marriage, he had a lot of
backgrounds to check out....

On the drive back from Gerry Smith's office, they decided that since they were entering this partnership "together," he might as well move into the bed-and-
breakfast for the two weeks before their wedding. Then,
thinking this as good a time as any, he casually asked

Savannah to let him meet her friends again and from the expression on her face he realized she suspected he was going to check them out. For a few seconds it appeared she might get angry, but, instead, she simply told him she would invite them to the house that night.

Within seconds after their arrival, he found himself seated on a stiff-backed chair across the sofa from four very curious, not-too-pleasant women, and for the first time since he made up his mind to interrogate them he wondered about the wisdom of it.

"So, Savannah tells me that she told you all the specifics of our marriage," he said, opening the conversation with truth since there was no way around it.

Not one of them smiled. Not one gave him an even semi-friendly look. His gaze moved from the two blue-eyed redheads to the blonde, to the last woman with the dark hair and serious eyes.

Though all four of them stared at him as if he were the angel of death, only Lindsay, the blonde, replied. "Yes. She told us that she was marrying you to preclude bad press which might hurt *your* father."

Though he tried to fight the ludicrous urge to defend himself, since it was her brother who had put them in this precarious position, he failed. "I could press charges against Barry, you know."

"Except that would be trouble for your father," Lindsay said. Her eyes were sharp, observant and her tone was clearly adversarial. If he were taking guesses, right now he would put money on the bet that this one would be an attorney someday.

"Yes, it would. But that doesn't negate the fact that I've made some concessions, too."

"Not as big as Savannah's concessions. If you look at this situation objectively," Lindsay said, "Savannah is giving up much more because she's forced to leave her home, which also happens to be her place of business, and ask her friends to run it while she's gone so she can live with you.''

"I don't mind," Savannah said, unexpectedly jumping into the conversation on his side.

Ethan cast her a sidelong glance, glad she spoke up. Her quick agreement proved she understood his logic, but it was also the first time they were on the same side. And it felt right. Good. Unfortunately, it also gave him a tingly feeling in the pit of his stomach, which he liked a little more than he should.

"Her living with me is the only way this really works.''

"That may be true," Becki said. "But I can't help but feel that you're somehow punishing Savannah for a crime her brother committed.''

Not one to let a good opportunity pass, Ethan leaped on that. "Which is my point exactly. Her brother is the one who committed this crime, but *my father* is the one who will suffer if word of this gets out. Can I trust you?'' he asked, looking from one woman to the next until he was sure he had their complete attention. "Can I trust that none of you will sell this story to a tabloid?''

Becki gasped, "Sell this story to a tabloid?''

"That's exactly what I said.''

"It appears, Mr. McKenzie," Andi said, "that you don't have a clue how friendship works.''

"I know how friendship works, but none of you is *my* friend. And it's my father who is in trouble. I need to know that I can trust you or there's no reason for Savannah and me to get married. And if there's no reason for Savannah and me to get married, all bets are off on this baby.''

Silence covered the room like a cloak. Though Ethan hadn't come right out and made a threat, everybody knew what he referred to when he said all bets are off on this baby. He glanced at Savannah, who sat perfectly still and silent. Though she wasn't trying to sway the opinion of the four women in her living room, she wasn't condemning *him*, either. She seemed to understand that he had no choice but to use the power at his disposal. And though she could have argued or cried, or even made her own threats, she did nothing. Said nothing. Which gave Ethan another odd tingly sensation. He wasn't sure if that was good or bad.

Finally, Mandi said, "We'll keep your secret, as long as you're fair with Savannah."

Ethan nodded. "I never had any intention of being anything but fair. But there's a lot at stake here, and I'm taking some pretty big chances, too. This is the deal Savannah and I struck. You guys are just going to have to trust me the same way she does."

Even as the words were coming out of his mouth, Ethan couldn't believe he said them. Not only had he admitted that he knew Savannah trusted him, and that's why she hadn't said or done anything when he made his threat, but also he had switched from making sure they kept the secret, to pleading his case because he wanted their approval. Why? Because it was obvious they loved Savannah and he didn't want them to worry about her.

"Does anybody want coffee?" Savannah asked, bouncing from her seat.

Ethan guessed she had done that hoping that if she disturbed the group at this point in the conversation they might consider it closed. And closed on a satisfactory ending—with him telling them they could trust him.

Since they had already said they would keep his secret, he couldn't think of a better way to end it himself.

"It's a little late in the day for coffee for me," Ethan said, doing his part to close the discussion. "But I wouldn't mind something cold."

"Neither would I," Becki said, rising. "Except you're not getting it," she added, nudging Savannah back down to her chair. "Mandi and I will get the drinks."

"Yeah, and Andi and I will get out the cards," Lindsay said, as she rose from the sofa. She looked at Ethan. "You do play poker?"

"I play poker," Ethan said cautiously.

"Good," Andi said, more or less directing everybody to a game table in the back of the room.

But when Andi and Lindsay were out of hearing distance, Savannah stopped Ethan by placing her fingers on his forearm. "You don't have to play. This is just how we amuse ourselves since Thurmont's not exactly a bustling metropolis."

"I don't mind," Ethan said, and realized that he didn't. Wacky thoughts were running through his mind. He had just butted heads with four women who should be thanking him for coming up with a plan that protected everybody, but he almost didn't care. The fierce loyalty Savannah inspired touched Ethan because he knew it proved something. Savannah Groggin was a genuinely good woman.

"Ethan?"

"Yes?" he said, then, forced out of his reverie, saw Andi was losing patience with waiting for him to accept the cards from her. Through the course of his musings, the sodas had been distributed, and everybody was waiting for him to deal.

"Sorry." He took the cards and began to shuffle, but

he couldn't stop his gaze from wandering over to Savannah. He should be pleased to constantly get confirmation of her virtue, but it only complicated the attraction he felt for her. He knew the genesis of his feelings was her pregnancy—because she was carrying his child he felt intimate with her. The puzzling, almost alarming part was that with confirmation came the realization that she was the same woman he had worked with two years ago. And realizing she was the same woman, he felt closer to her— which deepened the sense of intimacy.

Worse, as the intimacy deepened, his feelings about their impending marriage were changing. Suddenly he was thinking that it would be okay to sleep together…and he meant *sleep*, at least he had initially. He just wanted to lie cuddled together, with their baby between them. But that need was growing into a desire to touch all the wonderful velvet skin he had sampled when she let him touch her stomach to feel the baby…and more.

As the poker game progressed, he unsuccessfully tried to fight the sexual turn of his thoughts by taking them into neutral territory. He reminded himself that she was sweet and innocent and that this made her beautiful, and vulnerable in a way that hit him right in the heart, and he wanted to protect her. And that was bad.

Bad.

Bad.

Bad.

Because that meant his feelings were transcending typical lust and even infatuation and rolling into territory that could become love.

The only anchor he could mentally hold on to to save himself was that Savannah might not be drawing these same conclusions. But even if she was, if he didn't say something first, odds were she would keep her emotions to herself because she was shy.

Plus, theirs wouldn't be a real marriage. As long as he stopped entertaining these crazy ideas, there would be no inappropriate touching, so both of them would be safe.

That thought comforted him through the rest of the card game. It comforted him as he waved goodbye to her friends. It comforted him through the awkward minute when he insisted she go to bed and let him turn out the lights and lock the doors for her.

But when he was climbing the stairs to his room, congratulating himself on his determination to keep both of their hearts safe, he suddenly realized that he *would* be touching her. He *would* be kissing her, and he *would* be pretending to be madly in love with her every time he was around his parents, or in the public eye.

If he wanted his parents and the press to believe this was a love match, he was going to have to pretend to be in love with her, which included touching, kissing, living together, being friends, sharing a child.

Boy, he was in big trouble. He had a sneaking suspicion that Savannah Groggin was the one woman he could trust enough to really make another honest stab at marriage. Except he didn't want to make an honest stab at marriage. The first shot almost killed him. He didn't want to risk his heart or his sanity again.

And the whole heck of it was, he couldn't even run like hell in the opposite direction to protect himself as he promised himself he would do if he ever met another woman who tempted him to let his guard down.

In seven days, he would be married to her.

Chapter Three

Standing in the small alcove off to the right of the courtroom in which he and Savannah would get married, Ethan turned at the sound of a side door opening. When he saw his parents, Penny and Parker McKenzie, he drew in a quick breath.

"Mom! Dad!"

Josh Anderson, the coconspirator who had been pressed into service to be Ethan's best man, and Olivia Brady, Josh's fiancée, both froze in surprise.

"Ethan McKenzie," his mother scolded, sounding exactly as she had when he was ten. Slim and beautiful in her teal-blue suit, with her blond hair pulled in a severe chignon, Penny McKenzie looked every bit the part of a Washington hostess. "How could you possibly get married and not tell your parents?"

"I—I—I don't know," Ethan said, too shocked by their appearance to quickly come up with a suitable lie.

"Hilton told us about the baby," Ethan's father, Parker, said. In the sophisticated black suit that comple-

mented his salt-and-pepper hair, he looked as rich, powerful and polished as his wife. He reached around Ethan
to shake Josh's hand. "Hi, Josh, good to see you again.
Who is this?"

"This is my fiancée, Olivia," Josh said, as Olivia
stepped forward.

While Josh introduced Olivia, Ethan realized how odd
this relationship must look to his parents. Even Ethan had
never suspected Josh and his secretary had more than a
professional relationship, but it was clear now that they
loved each other and were happy. In spite of being
dressed in a tuxedo Josh was more relaxed than Ethan
had ever seen him, and Olivia, wearing a bright-red dress
that complemented her sunny yellow hair and peaches-
and-cream complexion, simply glowed.

"Nice to meet you, Olivia," Parker and Penny said,
both shaking Olivia's hand.

"Hilton also explained that when you told him your
girlfriend was pregnant," Penny said, picking up the account her husband had started. "He spilled the beans
about your father's impending vice presidential an-
nouncement, and the two of you realized you needed to
get married as soon as possible so the pregnancy didn't
detract from the campaign."

"And I appreciate that," Parker said sincerely, catching Ethan's gaze. "However, you still should have invited us to the wedding."

"I'm sorry, Dad," Ethan apologized contritely, but inside he was marveling at Hilton's brilliance. Having the
family friend leak that Ethan was getting married gave
the first breath of life to the story that would keep Parker's career safe, and Ethan's parents' involvement innocent. They were here, they were participating, but they
didn't really know anything. Yet they believed they were

privy to the bottom-line secrets. It would play perfectly in the press. "Everything just happened so fast—"

"Because you're going to have a baby!" Penny interrupted, reaching up to lay her palms on her son's cheeks. "My baby is going to have a baby."

Once again overcome with his own emotion about having a child, Ethan knew exactly what his mother was feeling. "I almost can't believe it myself, Mom."

"We couldn't be happier," she said, then hugged Ethan fiercely. "In this day and age, the timing means nothing. I'm glad you're not letting it concern you because it certainly doesn't concern us. I'm ready to shop for the nursery with your new wife...."

Ethan saw Olivia and Josh exchange a quick look and he knew why. The comment underscored the fact that Savannah was going to have to deal with Ethan's mother for the next few months, but more than that, it reminded Olivia and Josh—and now Ethan—of something they should have thought of from the minute they laid eyes on his parents. Savannah wasn't expecting to meet his famous family today. She was on the other side of the courtroom, in her new white suit, probably getting rid of last-minute jitters by talking with her friends, completely unsuspecting of her fate.

He prayed a silent prayer that she didn't mind surprises. "You're going to have to talk to Savannah about the nursery, but right now," he said, glancing at his watch, "you better go into the courtroom and take a seat. The judge will be here any minute. He said we'd start at three o'clock sharp and I have no reason to doubt him."

At that his mother's expression changed marginally. "Honey, did you hire a photographer?"

"No," Ethan said, glad that at least this much of his explanation wasn't a lie. "We threw this wedding together on short notice, Mom. Savannah and I figured we could pose for pictures at a studio later or you could have someone at the reception you're undoubtedly going to host.''

Penny had the good grace to laugh and not try to pretend she wasn't already planning some kind of party for the newlyweds. ''Studio photos are fine,'' she said. ''But I wanted pictures of the ceremony. I knew you were pressed for time. I also knew you weren't thinking about details, so I called someone. He's probably out front now.''

''Mom!'' Ethan gasped. Not only was he about to force Savannah to meet his family long before she was prepared, but he was also about to ask her to endure an impromptu photo session. ''I can't just...we can't just—''

''Savannah will be fine with it,'' Penny assured Ethan with feminine confidence. ''All women want photos of their wedding. Trust me, she will thank me.''

''Yeah, it's okay, Ethan,'' Olivia said, sending Ethan the message with her expression that it would be better for Ethan to trust that Savannah could handle this than to argue and raise his parents' suspicions.

''Okay,'' Ethan said.

''Now that that's settled...'' Josh said, taking over the way Ethan knew a best man was supposed to when the groom was nearly on the verge of panic from unexpected complications. ''Olivia, why don't you take Ethan's parents out to their seats and we'll catch up with all of you after the ceremony?''

''Great,'' Parker said. He held his wife's elbow to escort her to the courtroom and Olivia led them out the door.

When they were gone, Ethan sagged. "What the hell am I doing?"

"You're fixing a problem," Josh said simply. "Keeping a secret that needs to be kept."

"You see, that's just the trouble," Ethan said, pacing now. "For something that's supposed to be a secret, a hell of a lot of people are involved."

"Who?" Josh asked sweeping out his hand in a gesture of dismissal. "The only people who know are me, Hilton and a couple of Savannah's friends."

Ethan caught Josh's gaze. "And Olivia."

"Olivia is Savannah's friend. So she goes into that general category. But more than that if you hadn't found out the real details and told us, Olivia wouldn't know. When Savannah was in Atlanta three months ago and she started leaking bits and pieces of this story she didn't tell Olivia she was already pregnant. Olivia thought she was only considering the procedure not in Atlanta for an exam."

"Yeah, yeah, whatever," Ethan said, the speed of his pacing increasing.

"You're just nervous."

"Because I suddenly realize how much I'm asking of Savannah."

"From what I remember of her, Savannah is very resilient."

"She better be because I have a sneaking suspicion that my mother might have also called the press."

Josh burst out laughing.

"Oh, funny. Very, very funny!"

Before Ethan could have a full-scale tirade, the side door of the courtroom opened again. The judge's secretary poked her head in. "Judge Flenner says to tell you we're ready."

"Okay," Ethan said. He took a long breath and straightened his shoulders.

Josh slapped him on the back. "You'll be fine."

"It's not myself I'm worried about. My naked-in-the-tub-at-age-two photo was part of a roast for my father's fortieth birthday. Everything I have and own has been exposed."

"Except this."

Stopped by Josh's insight, Ethan looked at his friend. "Except this," he agreed quietly.

"And keeping this little slice of your life a secret depends on Savannah," Josh continued. "This is probably the first time in your life you've ever trusted anyone this completely."

Ethan shook his head. "No, I trusted my ex-wife completely. That's probably why I'm worried. She let me down."

"Well, Savannah's not going to let you down," Josh said, guiding Ethan to the courtroom.

Josh's last comment echoed in Ethan's head as he walked to the front of the judge's bench and during the entire time Savannah glided up the aisle. She wore a simple white suit with a short skirt that showcased her perfect legs—legs that he had really never noticed before, but couldn't help but admire now. Her jacket fit loosely around her waist and the voluminous bouquet of peach, yellow and white flowers was strategically placed in front of her tummy, so she didn't even look pregnant. Her red hair cascaded around her in loose, languid curls.

With every step she took, she looked more beautiful to Ethan. But also the closer she got the more he began to sense that Josh was right. And her friends were right. And even Ethan's own instincts were right. This was a woman he could trust. Though he had originally suggested this marriage as a way to protect his father, while he subtly kept an eye on Savannah and made sure she didn't get any blackmail ideas, he suddenly knew beyond a shadow of a doubt that he need not have worried. Savannah would never take advantage of this situation.

He could trust her.

She reached him and he held out his hand to her. Quivering with nerves she presented her hand and, on impulse, Ethan brought it to his lips and kissed her fingers. Because he knew her as a shy, sweet young woman, he knew this had to be difficult for her, yet she was performing like a trooper, holding up her end of the bargain with dazzling poise. He very much appreciated everything she was doing for him, and that was what he wanted to communicate with the quick brush of his lips. Instead, even to him, the gesture became inordinately romantic. Her lips lifted slightly acknowledging her pleasure from the caress, and their gazes met and clung.

Ethan wasn't really sure what they were telling each other, or looking for in the ten seconds they searched each other's eyes. He only felt an odd sense of assurance. He knew they were doing the right thing, and he knew she knew it, too. With this marriage, they were saving her brother, protecting his father and giving themselves the chance to get to know each other well enough that they could make the necessary decisions about the baby.

The sense of rightness strengthened Ethan's confidence, as he and Savannah faced the judge. The familiar words of the ceremony began to float into the echoing room, and with every phrase of their vows he felt better, safer, more in control of his world. Until he realized that the next statement in this very familiar service would be, "You may kiss the bride."

He thought the words one second before the judge said

them and all of his nerve endings crackled to life. But
not with fear, with confusion. This beautiful woman was
his bride. His *bride*. And it all felt so real. The marriage
felt real. The commitment felt real. Kissing her felt like
the right thing to do.

He reminded himself that it wasn't. In fact, respecting
her sensibilities, he knew he shouldn't really kiss her, just
brush her cheek with his lips. Unfortunately, with his
parents as an audience, Ethan knew he couldn't get away
without something substantial. He lowered his head and
touched his mouth to hers.

Lightning zinged through him—and the sense that they
belonged together returned full force. He convinced himself it was simply nerves, until he pulled back slightly
and he saw the same flash of recognition in Savannah's
eyes. It didn't matter that this wedding was staged to
solve a problem. For some darned reason or another, it
felt right.

Everything in the room, the judge, his parents, Savannah's friends, even the baby, disappeared from his mind
for a few seconds. He saw only the look in Savannah's
eyes. Serious. Intense. Curious.

It was the curiosity that caused him to lower his head
and kiss her again. He genuinely believed that the only
way to get to the bottom of this deal was to kiss her the
way a man kisses a woman who interests him, a woman
who attracts him. And that's what he did. With no regard
for place or time, he put his hands on the small of her
back and nudged her closer, even as he changed the kiss
from a tentative press to a gentle request that she yield
to him.

She did. With her hands creeping up to his shoulders,
she tilted her head back and her lips softened ever so
slightly, but offering enough of an opening that Ethan

could take full advantage. He forgot this was a pretend marriage. He forgot they were in front of a crowd. He forgot everything except that he was attracted to her, and he kissed her hungrily, greedily, eagerly.

His tongue tumbled into her mouth, seeking the warm, wet recesses. He stroked her, filled her, took everything she unselfishly gave and he felt himself falling over a precipice, headfirst into that sense of rightness he kept feeling. Soft and vulnerable, she clung to him, accepting everything, and kissing him back, making him feel as desirable to her as she was to him. His hands slid down the smooth column of her spine, then raced back up again, even as his mouth plundered hers. She tasted warm and sweet, yet he felt anything but sweet toward her. And that was exactly how she kissed him, as if she felt anything but sweet toward him.

The knowledge hitched his desire a notch and he deepened the kiss, pulling her even closer, squashing her bouquet of peach, yellow and white roses between them.

Judge Flenner cleared his throat. ''Okay, since the room is booked for another ceremony in fifteen minutes, I think I'm going to have to call a halt to this kiss.''

Ethan felt as if somebody had poured cold water on his head. The titter of laughter that ran through the group was like the second bucket. He stepped away, and for several seconds he and Savannah simply stared into each other's eyes, both of them immeasurably confused about what to do now. They weren't friends, but they weren't really strangers, either. Neither one of them could really say what they were. But whatever it was, whatever relationship had evolved out of proximity in the past two weeks, they now knew it was fraught with sexual chemistry.

Then he took her hand and turned her toward the waiting guests.

"I present Mr. and Mrs. Ethan McKenzie," Judge Flenner announced proudly.

And Ethan led Savannah down the aisle to meet his parents, tingling with arousal, attracted to a woman who seemed every bit as attracted to him, confused to the hilt about their relationship, and presented her as his bride.

After meeting *the* Parker and Penny McKenzie, and posing for an hour of photos, Savannah found herself in a limousine with Ethan and his parents. Luckily, the ride only seemed to take seconds with Parker and Penny chatting like two proud parents. In the restaurant, Savannah quietly took her seat beside Ethan at the round table in the private room. Though the guests were mostly her friends, and she even knew Josh and Olivia, two of the four people Ethan had invited, Savannah couldn't speak to save her soul. She was so angry she wanted to throw herself across her bed and weep.

She wasn't upset that Ethan's parents had come for the ceremony. She didn't even care that they had brought a photographer. From the way Josh told the story she understood bringing a private photographer to get appropriate pictures for a press release probably saved her from facing the actual press. What bothered her was that kiss.

She'd never been kissed so thoroughly or so deliciously and she sincerely doubted she ever would be again. The kiss was wonderful and magical and Savannah wanted to scream and rail at Ethan for it because it ruined everything. He kissed her the way a man truly kissed his bride. In doing that he took a pretend ceremony and nudged it into the realm of reality, because he'd forced them to admit that they were attracted to each other enough that they could develop real feelings for each other.

And that would be a disaster. Because she couldn't fall in love with him. All she had to do was look around the private room and watch the interplay between his parents and the waitstaff of the small Thurmont restaurant—who at present were nearly scraping and bowing with respect and awe over their guests—and Savannah knew she didn't fit in to Ethan's world. He might be temporarily infatuated because she was pregnant with his child, but if she fell in love with him, he would hurt her.

She knew it as surely as she knew her first, middle and last names. If she let herself fall, she would be signing up for six months of dark depression and misery when he realized he didn't love her, only loved that she was having his baby.

Through dinner, she kept herself cool and aloof. She was appropriately happy and bubbly with his parents. She was warm with her own friends. She heartily congratulated newly engaged Josh and Olivia, who Savannah knew would be blissfully happy for the rest of their lives, but she wouldn't, couldn't, speak two words to Ethan.

After their meal, Ethan whisked Savannah out of the restaurant with the explanation to their guests that he thought the day had been too much excitement for her. Because she hadn't argued, and instead had apologized for needing to leave early, he knew he had guessed correctly in thinking she wanted to go home. He suspected her mood had more to do with confusion over that kiss than being tired, but he also knew they couldn't discuss it until they were alone.

Luckily it was only a little after nine when he unlocked the door to the bed-and-breakfast and escorted her inside.

He didn't give her a chance to run up the stairs, but caught her hand and pulled her into the all-blue living room.

"We have to talk about this."

"No, I don't think we do."

"Savannah, it's obvious that you're furious with me, and I don't have a clue why." And he didn't. Before he kissed her the second time he saw in her eyes that she wanted to test their attraction as much as he did. Now they knew there was something more between them than the baby. It scared him.

"You don't have a clue?" Savannah said, staring at him with her huge green eyes. "Ethan, you kissed me as if you were going to make love to me right there in front of the judge."

Again, clueless about why that would make her this *angry,* he groped for the only logical explanation that came into his mind and said, "I'm sorry if I embarrassed you."

"You didn't embarrass me. You broke our pact," she said as he directed her to sit on the sofa.

He sat beside her. "What pact?"

"That we would have a marriage in name only."

"I don't remember making that pact."

"You did," she insisted. "You said that though we had to pretend to be a love match for your parents, you wouldn't fawn all over me or expect me to be your wife for real."

"Ah."

"And now I feel like you're going back on that deal."

"What if I am?" Ethan asked, stretching his arms across the back of her sofa. "Is it so wrong for me to want to make love to you?"

His words sent a little shiver up her spine because his

wanting to make love to her was exactly the problem. She could see the desire in his eyes and it struck a chord in her. No one had ever kissed her the way Ethan had, which made it an easy leap to realize no one had ever wanted her the way Ethan seemed to. Not only was this new for her, but it puzzled her. He could have any woman he wanted. Why her?

She had red hair, freckles. There was nothing special about her. Except that he wanted her because she was pregnant with his child. When the baby was born and he had his son or daughter, the bubble would burst.

"The truth is I don't trust these feelings you suddenly have," Savannah said, forcing herself to swallow an unexpected lump of pain. She didn't believe he loved her and she knew darned well she didn't love him. She had only been personally involved with him for two weeks. She couldn't love him. Not yet. And he couldn't love her.

"Why not?" Again his words were spoken with quiet male confidence. But more than that, he reached out and took a lock of her hair and began twining it around his finger.

"Because we don't know each other. Because I think you're feeling all these emotions for me because I'm having your baby," she whispered, as shivers of the beginnings of arousal resonated through her. He was trying to make her believe this could be simple but she knew better. Every time she loved somebody she lost them. Boyfriends broke up with her. Her parents were dead. Even her brother was lost to her because he had gone into hiding. She wouldn't take a chance with her heart when the cards were so clearly stacked against her.

"Right now," she said, swallowing tears, "you think you feel things for me...and you do," she hastily assured him. Not wanting to insult him or offend him since they had four long months to live together, she caught his gaze. Then she wished she hadn't. He looked at her intently, desire shining from the depths of his dark eyes. They were so bright they seemed to be picking up the glow of the lamplight and reflecting it. It was plain that he truly believed he wanted her. And Savannah acknowledged he might...sexually. But she couldn't settle for that. No matter how tempting.

"Ethan, four months from now, after this baby is born, can you tell me you will feel the same way?"

He didn't answer, but Savannah didn't give him a long space of time to come up with a legitimate debate. She rose from the sofa.

"Let me make this simple for both of us. I don't want to fall in love with you. I don't want you falling in love with me. We made a deal. I want to stick to it."

"Okay," Ethan said, then immediately glanced away from her as if the decision had been of no consequence. He shifted on the sofa to get more comfortable as he reached for a magazine she had lying on the table for guests. He didn't look at her. He didn't argue with her. He hardly seemed to care.

His easy acceptance insulted her as much as his pushing the envelope with their kiss because it reinforced that he didn't have feelings for her only felt a sexual attraction and, irrationally, that hurt. It nearly forced the tears hovering on her lashes to spill onto her cheeks.

"Okay," she said and left the room to go to her bedroom, tears clinging to her eyelashes and closing her throat.

Ethan listened to the sounds of her climbing the stairs but didn't move. He wanted her enough that he would never in a million years agree to stick to a bargain made fourteen days ago when the intervening two weeks had changed everything between them. He was attracted to her, aroused, and could see she felt the same way about him. And, for Pete's sake they were married. He was sure they could have had the most explosive wedding night in recorded history…except there were tears in her eyes.

Savannah said she didn't want to fall in love with him or to have him fall in love with her. Though her words dented his ego, he rationalized that choice as a result of her fear about his parents, his life, his lifestyle. But that was something they could deal with, not a reason to stay away from each other. He genuinely believed they could and should have the healthy sexual relationship that seemed so obvious.

Except there were tears in her eyes and he couldn't handle that he had hurt her, or that she feared he was about to hurt her—particularly since he had made a mission out of protecting his own heart.

He not only understood her fear of getting involved, he also empathized. Because he felt what she felt, he had to agree.

Chapter Four

On Monday morning, Savannah was just getting out of the shower of the suite Ethan had given her in his home, when she was summoned by a maid who told her she had visitors in the living room. After towel-drying her hair and quickly dressing in jeans and a big T-shirt, she stepped into Ethan's formal living room to find Gina Martin, daughter of Hilton Martin, and Olivia Brady standing by the traditional style floral sofa. Olivia obviously held back a laugh as Gina stared at Savannah's stomach incredulously.

"Oh, my gosh!"

"Hi!" Savannah said, happy to see two friendly faces. Saturday she married Ethan. Sunday she gave final instructions to her friends about how to run the bed-and-breakfast. And Sunday night she was on her way to a new world. A new life. A new everything.

"Why aren't you two at work?"

"I'm not working full-time anymore..." Olivia began, but still caught up in seeing Savannah pregnant, Gina, a five foot seven, sable-haired bundle of energy, propelled herself at Savannah and enveloped her in a hug.

"I'm so happy for you."

"Well, I'm so happy for me, too," Savannah said honestly, because if nothing else she was happy about her baby. "Come in, Ethan's around here somewhere. I'll get him."

Gina caught her wrist. "No! Absolutely not! I want to hear every detail of this romance that I knew nothing about."

"There's really not much to tell," Savannah said, indicating with a wave of her hand that Gina and Olivia should take a seat on the sofa as she sat on the chair across from it. Finished with cherrywood accents of end tables, bookcases, curio cabinets and credenzas, Ethan's living room was neat without being fussy. Like the rest of the huge home, the décor spoke of wealth, but not extravagance.

"We met one day by accident," she continued, "and kind of started seeing each other."

"Kind of started seeing each other?" Gina said with a laugh, her violet-blue eyes dancing with mirth. "Look at you!" she said pointing at Savannah's stomach. "You did more than kind of start seeing each other."

"It was a case of love at first sight," Ethan said, strolling into the room, and just like it did every time she saw him, Savannah's heart flip-flopped. He wore a dark suit, white shirt and print tie and looked so smart, sophisticated and handsome Savannah was surprised her breath didn't catch.

Olivia continued to hold back her laughter, and Gina stared dumbfounded at Ethan as he walked across the room and bent to kiss Savannah's forehead. A shiver ran through her at the simple brush of his lips, and though her real need was to cry at the injustice of being forced to be so close to someone she wanted but couldn't have, she smiled up at him. "Are you leaving for work?" she asked, trying to sound like a loving wife.

"Are you okay?" Ethan countered. Though it appeared to their guests he was inquiring about her health, his expression actually asked if she needed help keeping the story straight with Gina.

She nodded her head. "I'm fine."

"Are you sure?"

She nodded again. She didn't like lying to Gina, and though Ethan, Hilton, Josh and Olivia felt the same way, they also knew keeping the truth from Gina was the best way to keep it from the press. Hilton had decided that if they could keep it from his daughter, they could keep it from anybody.

"I'm fine."

"Okay, then, I'll see you for lunch."

"You don't have to come home for lunch," Savannah said with a laugh. Recognizing it might be best to have this chat by the door, away from Gina's prying eyes and Olivia's muffled giggles, she attempted to push herself up from the chair and immediately Ethan offered his hand to assist her. The simple gesture, so quick, so generous, so sincere reminded her again that he really was a sweet guy, and made her feel terrible for placing all the blame for that kiss on him. She knew they couldn't sleep together. She didn't like that he wanted to change their deal. But she had participated in that kiss as much as he had, yet she didn't take her end of the responsibility because she was afraid that if she admitted her feelings for him he could talk her into anything.

When they got to the door, Ethan immediately put his arms around her and pulled her close. "They can see here from the sofa,'' he whispered before brushing his lips across her forehead again.

Though Savannah's fondest wish was to apologize for their wedding night, she knew that would only complicate things so she said, ''I'm sorry. I'll get better at this.''

''You're doing fine, Savannah,'' Ethan assured her.

She drew a long breath. ''I hope so.''

''I know so. Is there anywhere special you would like to go for lunch?''

''No. In fact, I don't think you should take me to lunch. I know we're supposed to be newlyweds, but you just missed two weeks of work. I think it will look odd if you don't try to catch up.''

He smiled down at her. ''Are you calling me a workaholic?''

''Yes.''

''Really?''

''You don't know that you are?'' Savannah asked, chuckling, realizing she was enjoying herself. Caught in the circle of his arms, steeped in his nearness, she was more relaxed than she had been in years. And though taking pleasure from being with him was nice, it wasn't really wise.

''No. I did not know that I was.''

She tried to step away, but he wouldn't let her. ''Well, you are and you better get to work or everybody will suspect something is wrong.''

''Won't they just think I'm in love?''

She almost said ''I wish,'' and caught herself just in time. She couldn't wish for Ethan to be in love with her. Even if she disregarded her fear that he wouldn't want her after the baby was born, they came from two different worlds and she didn't fit into his. After only twenty-four hours in his house, she wasn't even sure she wanted to fit. Being in love, for real, would be a disaster.

"No, they'll think you've lost your mind," she said, then stepped back attempting again to get out of his arms. Because he wouldn't release her, she sighed. "Go to work."

"Okay," he said, but he peered into her eyes for a few seconds as if gauging something, then bent his head and kissed her.

It was the first time he'd kissed her since the kiss after their vows and Savannah knew why he'd hesitated. Not only had the first kiss upset her, but they definitely had some kind of chemistry between them. Smart people would avoid this at all costs, and when forced to kiss they had best realize they were playing with fire.

Because they were. The second his lips touched hers, Savannah felt hot inside and out. Warmth seemed to radiate from him to her, but more than that the smooth wetness of his lips called to her. He kissed her gently, as if deadly aware that the wrong move would ignite sparks, but in its very tenderness the kiss was even more explosive than the passionate one of two days ago. He made her feel loved, cherished and special. He made her want to melt into his arms and stay there forever.

She pushed out of his hold and immediately looked away. "I'll see you at about six then."

"Yeah," he said, his voice a husky whisper. "I've given the staff instructions for dinner, and I also told them that you would be talking with them today about any changes you want made in how things run around here."

Her eyes shot upward and she caught his gaze. "I don't want to make any changes."

"Savannah, you may not like the cleaning schedules.

You may discover that the cupboards don't have the foods you like. You might want more towels. You might be allergic to the detergent. There are a hundred things you might want done differently.''

She swallowed. ''Maybe.''

''Just relax today. Enjoy your time with Gina and Olivia. You and I can talk with the staff tonight.''

Feeling witless and unsophisticated, she bit her lower lip. ''Okay.''

''Okay,'' he said, then lifted her chin until she looked at him. ''You'll be fine.''

She managed a smile. ''Sure. I'm just a little uneasy because all this is new.''

''That's normal. We can handle that.''

After he left, Savannah took a minute to compose herself before she returned to the living room where she found Gina bursting with questions and Olivia giving her a curious look.

''Things appeared to be getting a little steamy out there,'' Olivia observed casually, but Savannah could tell from the tone of Olivia's voice that she was falling into the same trap Savannah was. She was starting to believe the lie.

''It's hard to get steamy when you look like this,'' Savannah said, pointing to her tummy as she slowly made her way to her chair, trying to remind Olivia of the reason she and Ethan got married, so she would remember there was no real relationship.

But though Savannah had thought her comment enough of a joke to stop Olivia's mind from racing and to confuse Gina, Gina didn't take it as funny. She jumped off the sofa and ran to the chair in which Savannah sat. ''Oh, honey, you look great! Pregnancy really agrees with you. And any fool can see Ethan loves you,'' she said, sitting on the arm of the chair so she could put her arm around Savannah. "He's just a very private person. He always has been. We didn't even know he was dating anybody that's how private he is about things."

"I know you're right," Savannah said, angry with herself because in trying to correct Olivia's impression she had upset Gina. And she knew why. It hurt that she and Ethan couldn't have a relationship because she liked him. Obviously, that disappointment had come through in her voice.

She drew a quick breath. "I'm sorry, guys. I don't mean to be so emotional. I think this is just hormones."

"Good, because Ethan's mother called me yesterday and she put me in charge of your reception."

"She did?" Savannah asked dismayed, though deep down inside she understood why Penny had done that, and it was the confirmation she needed to hear to get herself on the right track and stop wishing that Ethan would love her. Because it didn't matter if he loved her. They didn't belong together. Even Ethan's mother didn't trust her with planning her own reception.

Again, Gina must have heard something in Savannah's tone because she said, "Now, don't get upset. This is a party she and her husband are giving for you. You're the honored guest. You're not supposed to plan it. The party is also to be held at my dad's house. That's why I'm in charge. But since I'm a sweet, wonderful woman who wants everything to be perfect for her friends..." she said, making Olivia laugh and Savannah smile ruefully. "I would like your input."

"I thought you said I wasn't supposed to plan it."

"You're not. I am. I'm the one who's going to get the caterer, order the flowers and choose the orchestra. But I thought it might be nice for you to pick the color scheme, have a part in the menu and have your choice of flowers."

The enthusiasm in Gina's voice touched a chord in Savannah and her interest blossomed. "I can have anything I want?"

"My father said money is no object."

"Ooohhhh," Olivia gasped. "You think your dad will do that for Josh and me?"

Gina peered at Olivia. "Have you set a date?"

Olivia blushed. "We're thinking fall."

"Good, I love a fall wedding. Get back to me when you really have set a date."

Savannah only stared at Gina. "Have you ever thought that you should be a wedding coordinator rather than a human resources director?"

"A million times a day I've thought I should be anything but a human resources director. But we'll talk about me another time. This morning I want at least a color scheme, flower choice and tentative menu. The party is one week from Saturday. We can't drag our feet."

"One week from Saturday!"

"Savannah, you are pregnant. We would like to have the reception without worrying that you'll go into labor."

"Good point," Olivia said.

"Yeah, good point," Savannah said but the reminder of the baby brought her back to reality again. Ethan hadn't married her because he loved her and though she was getting the choice of anything she wanted for this fabulous reception, it felt irrational to be excited about a wedding that was fake. Yet she was, and she knew why she was. No matter how hard she tried to keep her perspective, she couldn't because she liked Ethan, and she wanted him to like her. And with her hormones raging the way they were this morning, she couldn't seem to shake the sadness.

Gina unexpectedly took Savannah's hands. "Savannah, remember when you were a little kid and you went swimming?"

Savannah nodded.

"Remember how some people were jumpers, some were waders? The jumpers never felt the chill. They just jumped in and started swimming. The waders shivered and grumbled," Gina observed.

"And made everything worse," Olivia agreed.

"Jump into this with both feet, Savannah, and things will go a lot easier."

Savannah nodded. Under normal circumstances she would agree. But the thing that Gina didn't know was that if Savannah jumped in, if she took on this role with the gusto that it required, she would fall in love with her pretend husband and leave this little play with a broken heart. She remembered her last broken heart too well to repeat it.

But, oddly enough, the reminder of her last relationship made her realize Gina was right. Except, she didn't need help fitting in to Ethan's life, she needed help keeping her perspective. If she used the swimming pool analogy to get that help, jumping in with both feet would mean entrusting Ethan with the truth of her life—gathering her courage and explaining the real truth of why she couldn't love him.

When Ethan arrived home that night the house was quiet. After putting his briefcase in the den, he went in search of Savannah. But he couldn't find her, and none of the staff seemed to know her whereabouts. Methodically, he went through each room and even looked in her private suite. Finally, he realized where she was and found her in the empty space he had told her he would soon be turning into a nursery.

"Hey."

She turned to face him and smiled. "Hey."

"Got any good suggestions for the nursery?"

"I think your decorating will depend on whether this is a boy or a girl."

"*Our* decorating. Savannah, anything to do with this child includes both of us."

She nodded. "I know."

He saw tears gathering in her eyes again and though she always used the convenient excuse of hormones to make him think nothing serious was wrong, her tears affected him like nothing ever affected him before. He didn't want her upset about anything. He didn't want her unhappy. Now that he knew he had nothing to fear from her, he recognized and acknowledged that he owed her because this scheme benefited him much more than it benefited her. She was doing him and his family an enormous favor. Not just in marrying him to keep the secret of his child's conception, but also in giving him a child. Because she never asked, he would gladly give her half of everything he owned. But she didn't ask, and he knew she never would. So her tears were like torture to him.

"Savannah, I know we threw you into a real pit of trouble here," he said, walking into the soon-to-be nursery and putting his hands on her shoulders. "But I didn't intend for you to be unhappy. So anything you want— anything—you just tell me and it's yours."

"Well, first of all you could start off by not being so nice to me."

He laughed, but when he looked into her sad green eyes, his laughter stopped. "You're serious."

She nodded.

"Savannah, I have to be nice to you. And not just for the charade. You're the mother of my child. I'd buy you a small island if I thought that would make you happy."

She shrugged out of his hold. "Don't."

He peered at her, more convinced than ever that she wasn't after anything but her brother's reprieve, and more confused than ever because his willingness to give her anything was proof that he trusted her. That alone should make her happy, not sad. "Don't?"

"Don't be so nice."

"Savannah, I'm really at a loss here."

She drew a long breath and paced to the window. Because she wouldn't look at him Ethan knew that what she was about to tell him was of monumental importance. So, he didn't push her. He waited.

"I might have been a little too flippant when I described my reasons for using in vitro fertilization to get pregnant."

"Oh?"

"Yeah," she said, her voice wobbling a little. "The truth is I lost my parents and moved to their B & B away from everybody and everything I knew in Atlanta, and sort of went into an enormous depression."

"I would think that would be normal."

She nodded, but still wouldn't look at him. "I thought so, too."

"But…"

"But I met someone. I fell head over heels in love…probably too quickly because of the loneliness in my life, and suddenly one day he just broke up with me."

"I'm sorry." Remembering the pain and sadness of her recent past, he was beginning to understand why money and things meant so little to her.

She peeked at him. "It gets worse," she said, then faced the window again. "About two weeks after he broke up with me, I had a false positive on a pregnancy test. I called him. He said we would get married and then I got my period, took the test again and realized I wasn't pregnant."

"And?"

"And he broke up with me and I was alone again."

With this much-needed insight into why she was so unhappy, he urgently said, "Savannah, I'm not going to desert you."

She turned again. Faced him. She studied him for several seconds before she said, "The problem is not you, Ethan, the problem is me. I'm really starting to like you."

"And this is bad because?" he asked teasingly.

She drew a long breath. "Because in a few months, after the baby is born, we are getting divorced. We will always be connected by this baby and I want us to remain on good terms. For the baby's sake, I want us to be really good friends. So I can't fall in love with you and have you hurt me."

Though he knew it was absolutely the wrong time to have this reaction, Ethan felt complimented that she was genuinely concerned about falling in love with him. And he knew she was because he could hear it in her voice. She honestly felt she could fall in love with him. Which was why she had warned him off on their wedding night and why she was warning him off now.

But Ethan forced his ego to take a back seat for a minute, walked over to the window, and turned her to face him. For several seconds he looked down into her liquid eyes, and degree by degree the intuition that had been nagging at him for days turned into realization. He was profoundly affected by her admission of affection because he had feelings for her, too. Real feelings. Important feelings. Not merely sexual attraction.

"Maybe the deal here, Savannah, is that we might not end up getting a divorce." He made the comment slowly, carefully, then combed his fingers through the silken tresses at her temples all the while watching the expression in her eyes. Just the touch of his fingers in her hair caused the green orbs to soften with emotion. "Maybe if we would both relax, this might work out."

With his hands in her hair, he bent his head and kissed her as gently and tenderly as he had ever kissed anyone. Not just because she was sad and vulnerable, but because that was how he felt about her. No one had ever been so important to him or so special.

But he forgot that no one aroused him as quickly and as potently as Savannah did, either, and a kiss that started off slow and tender, quickly tumbled into something hot and passionate.

Savannah pushed out of his arms. "Don't!" she said, nearly shouting from emotion. "What I am trying to tell you is that I have been hurt, and I don't want to take a chance on falling in love again. If I really wanted a relationship, don't you think I could have waited a few months or a year, gotten involved again, and had a child the normal way?"

Her question took him by surprise, but also forced him to face something he had been missing. There *was* a reason she had used in vitro fertilization. And it wasn't to get *his* child. It was to get the child of someone she didn't know. Someone who didn't know her. Instead, because she bore the child of someone she knew, someone she had to help, she was giving up the one thing she really wanted. The right to have and raise this child alone, without the pains and burdens of the romantic relationship that typically accompanied motherhood. By getting caught, her brother had screwed up her plan royally.

Looking at her fabulous hair, her lips still moist from his kiss, her angelic face, Ethan said, "Yes, I know that if you had wanted things to be different, you definitely could have had another relationship."

"But I didn't want one. Especially not with someone like you. No offense," she said, trying to soften the blow and failing miserably because every word she said had attacked him like a schoolyard bully. "But you and I aren't even in the same league. Your family is important and wealthy. I've never even been noticed by anyone let alone had my name in the paper until I married you. I always just make it financially. You're rich beyond what I can even imagine."

With that she started to pace. "We're probably going to want to raise the child differently. There are so many problems that something is bound to separate us and I can't risk getting hurt again. I have been there before, not just with my former boyfriend, but also with my parents. I know how hard it is to bring myself back to life when I lose somebody I love. I will not go through it again."

With that, she turned and left and Ethan stood in the echoing silence of the empty nursery. He was angry. Really, really angry. And he wasn't even sure why. He could have thought it was because most women would jump at the chance to go out with him, and the one he was starting to care for didn't want him. But he wouldn't let himself get away with a flippant answer. Because he liked her, he had to be honest and admit she was right. They were not suited to each other, and pretending they were was nothing but stupid.

Or maybe wishful thinking.

Chapter Five

For the next few days, Ethan was quiet and sullen, but Savannah decided that was better than sweet because when he was sweet it was too tempting to lean on him and appreciate him, and she couldn't do that. She didn't have a lot of people in her life. She had always wanted more. In a lot of ways she *needed* more people. Even if she and Ethan didn't become lovers, if Ethan simply endeared himself to her, it would be painful to separate when they divorced. And they had to divorce. She didn't fit in his life. There was no point in pretending there would be a fairy-tale ending for them. It wasn't going to happen.

By Friday he had gone from moody to reasonable, and on Saturday he was agreeable without going overboard. So, on Sunday morning when he came to breakfast in the formal dining room—the room with the long mahogany table and the kind of china Savannah had only seen in a jewelry store—looking like he was ready to choke someone, she had no clue why.

"Savannah," he said, only acknowledging her presence, his tone clipped and impersonal as he yanked out his chair and seated himself.

"I hope you don't mind," Savannah ventured uncertainly, positive he had to be angry because she had begun eating breakfast without him. "But I thought that since it was Sunday you would like to sleep late. I was starving so I started without you."

For a second, concern for her softened his sharp brown eyes, but only for a second. "I'm glad you began without me if you were starving," he said, snapping open his napkin.

"Okay," she said, curious now about why he could be so angry since she hadn't said enough to him in the past week to raise any kind of ire. "Then I don't have any idea why you're so mad."

"Really?" he said, turning as a cheerful maid entered. Young, no more than twenty-two, with light brown hair pulled into a tight bun, and wearing a pink uniform, Joni Carter stopped at Ethan's left, but didn't say anything.

"Eggs, toast, coffee," he said, and though not rude, he certainly wasn't polite. The young woman nodded her understanding, then fled as if unaccustomed to this temper from her employer.

"Really. I have no idea," she said, ready to turn and run herself because this dark mood scared even her. She didn't think that he would hurt her, but she also couldn't see herself living with a brooding, angry man for another five months.

"Well, why don't we try this on for size? My attorney called me this morning. He tells me that the clinic approached him to get me to sign an authorization giving my permission to release my end of the records of your procedure because your attorney approached them."

"Oh," Savannah said, sighing with understanding and relief. "Ethan, I'm not doing anything illegal. My brother has a right to see the proof of what he's accused of doing!"

"Nothing!" Ethan thundered. "He's accused of nothing, because I'm not pressing charges!"

"And it upsets you that we're going through the motions as if you were filing charges?"

"Did it ever occur to you that I might take this as your first step to wrangling out of our agreement? That it seems to me that you're trying to make a case to wiggle out of this."

Savannah gasped. "No! Ethan, no! I made a deal. I'm going to keep it. You have nothing to worry about."

He looked her right in the eye. "Don't I?"

"No," Savannah whispered. Now that she understood his anger, she realized he had a right to it. She might not have gone after those records to wiggle out of their deal, but she had gone after them to ensure she didn't lose custody of the baby. Though her friends wouldn't let her use the word blackmail, her motives were not pure. She swallowed. "I'm sorry."

Calmer now, he took a long, slow breath. "You should have told me."

"Yes, I should have."

"So why didn't you?"

For a few seconds, she toyed with her silverware and didn't look at him. She couldn't tell him the truth of why she had sought those papers and why she hadn't discussed getting them with him, because he would be even angrier. Particularly since, having met Penny and Parker McKenzie and knowing Ethan better, she understood his family wouldn't do something like that to her or the child. And, realizing that, she suddenly felt very unsophisticated and very, very foolish.

"All I was doing was a little background check. Just trying to make sure that everything was as it appeared, that's all."

"Savannah," Ethan said, his patience deteriorating again. "What you were doing was checking up on me. Making sure what I told you was the truth."

It might not have been appropriate to get the papers for blackmail, but even to someone unsophisticated it didn't seem out of line to want to confirm the facts. "And you blame me for that?"

"It makes me feel that you don't trust me."

"I *do* trust you, Ethan," Savannah said, sympathetic to his anger, but also feeling she was within her rights to have done what she did. "But I didn't and don't trust this situation. I think I had a right to at least see the preliminary information for myself."

"Well, you will be seeing it. I'm having them fax a medical release to me so that I can sign it and all the paperwork can be turned over to your attorney. God forbid you should take my word."

With that he threw his napkin on the table and stormed out. Savannah sat in the silent room, the heat of embarrassment suffusing her, along with the chill of remorse. The combination was nearly overwhelming, as the diametrically opposed, complex emotions poured through her.

Her primary purpose might have been to keep her baby, but she also wanted to know the truth, the entire truth. She did not think she was wrong to ask to see the paperwork. At the time, it seemed like the right thing to do. Even now, she recognized she would do it again if put in the situation of marrying a man she didn't really know, except as a boss.

The young maid entered, carrying Ethan's breakfast and Savannah smiled sheepishly. ''I'm sorry. He's gone.''

Joni looked as if she was going to turn away, but thought the better of it and faced Savannah again. Softly, kindly, she said, ''Whatever it was, you should have told him.''

''Yeah,'' Savannah agreed, nodding ruefully. ''But hindsight is always twenty-twenty.''

''Yes, ma'am,'' the maid said before turning with Ethan's breakfast and pushing through the swinging door into the kitchen.

Again Savannah was left to sit in the thick silence of the empty room. She didn't want to fall in love with Ethan, but she hadn't intended to make him an enemy, either.

The young maid entered the dining room again. ''Will there be anything else, ma'am?''

''No,'' Savannah said, smiling at Joni before she scampered from the room.

Savannah sunk in her seat. The tension between her and Ethan was now her fault, but she didn't know how to fix it. She couldn't even think of a nice thing to do to make it up to him. She couldn't call Gina for advice. She wasn't in on the secret. She wouldn't call Olivia on a Sunday morning when she had only recently discovered the love of her life and was probably still in bed. And she didn't think her Maryland friends could help her with this one, if only because they didn't know Ethan or anybody like him.

Staring at the discreet swinging door that connected the dining room to the kitchen, Savannah was suddenly inspired. Beyond that door were at least two people who knew her husband very, very well. They fixed his meals. They cleaned his home. They washed his clothes.

Surely, they knew something about his likes and dislikes.

Without thought for propriety or possible consequences, she rose and made her way into the austere black-and-white kitchen. The cook, Mrs. Perez, stood by the polished chrome stove, drinking a cup of coffee. Joni sat on a tall stool at the counter, eating the breakfast Ethan had left behind. Both froze when they saw her.

"Mrs. McKenzie!"

"It's all right," Savannah said, waving her hands to indicate they could continue with what they were doing when she arrived. "I don't need anything except a little information."

The cook, a woman in her late fifties who didn't seem to appreciate the intrusion into her domain, gave Savannah a narrow-eyed look. "What kind of information?"

"I had a disagreement with Mr. McKenzie."

The maid and the cook exchanged a glance.

"We heard," Mrs. Perez said.

Joni nodded. "I've never seen Mr. McKenzie this angry with anyone," she said, shoving aside Ethan's breakfast as if it didn't interest her as much as this possible conversation. "Actually, I've never seen him angry at all."

"Neither have I," Savannah agreed.

"He's a good man to work for," the cook said, still eyeing Savannah cautiously. "That's why we don't like to see him mad."

"I don't like to see him mad, either. I want to do something to make it up to him."

"Like what?" Mrs. Perez asked.

"I don't know. Have you ever seen anything his other girlfriends did for him?"

The older woman pushed out a laugh as if Savannah were crazy to ask. "Even if I did, I wouldn't be allowed to tell you."

"No, I guess not."

"You don't know a whole hell of a lot about this world, do you?" Mrs. Perez asked, walking over to pour herself another cup of coffee.

"No. I don't," Savannah said, grimacing. "Does it show that much. I mean, do I look like that awful of a wife?"

"No. You look like a sad wife," Joni said, then her gaze shot over to Mrs. Perez as if she were afraid to have spoken out of turn.

"It's all right. I am sad."

Mrs. Perez sighed, giving in. "We think that's why Mr. McKenzie is so easy to upset lately. We think that's why he yelled at you today. He's not the kind of guy who goes around hurting people. Just the opposite. Yet it seems like no matter what he does he can't please you."

"Actually, he's doing just fine at pleasing me. Some days he even goes too far," Savannah said, running her fingers through her long hair. "And that's usually when we fight. This time, though, I did something wrong and I have to figure out what to do to make it up to him." When neither Joni nor Mrs. Perez said anything, she smiled ruefully. "I'm sorry. I probably shouldn't be telling you this."

The cook sighed again before venturing back to the stove. She didn't meet Savannah's eyes when she said, "It's okay. We all see you have no one else to talk to."

Savannah nodded regretfully, but Joni perked up.

"You know, since Mr. McKenzie missed his breakfast, if you wanted to make this up to him, you could probably take something into the office for him to eat."

Liking the sound of that because it served a dual purpose—feeding Ethan the breakfast he missed, and building a bridge—Savannah faced Joni. "Do we have a picnic basket?"

Joni grinned. "What we don't have we can get here in twenty minutes. We have contacts who have contacts."

"Even on a Sunday morning?"

"Piece of cake."

"Good. Then I want a picnic lunch. It will take me at least an hour to get dressed and an hour to drive through traffic to get to Hilton-Cooper-Martin Foods, so by that time lunch will be more in order."

"That's the spirit," Joni said as she walked to the sink to rinse her breakfast dishes. "You get dressed and leave the lunch to us." She paused in her rinsing, glanced at Mrs. Perez as if seeking approval then faced Savannah. "By the way, you won't be driving in."

"I won't?"

"No," Mrs. Perez said firmly, finally really joining the conversation. "Because you're pregnant and you've been out of Atlanta for so long you probably forgot how to drive in our traffic, if I were you I would take a car and have Lewis drive me. I think," Mrs. Perez said, smiling conspiratorially at Savannah, "Mr. McKenzie would appreciate the gesture."

"I think you're right," Savannah agreed. Buoyed with enthusiasm, Savannah ran upstairs, showered and dressed in a pretty pink sundress and sandals. When she arrived downstairs both Lewis and the basket were waiting.

* * *

When Savannah appeared at his office door, Ethan gasped with alarm. "What are you doing here?"

"Relax," she said, strolling into his office with Lewis behind her carrying a picnic basket. "I brought the cavalry."

"So I see," Ethan said, taking his seat behind the desk again because he was curious. Not only had she come to the office, with a gift, which he took as an apology, but she had befriended his household staff to do it. "Is that lunch?"

"Joni thought it should have been breakfast since you left yours sitting."

Ethan bit back a smile. *Joni?* It appeared she hadn't merely befriended his staff, she seemed to be on a casual first-name basis with at least one of them. "I was a little angry."

"And now?"

"Maybe it depends on what's in that basket," Ethan said, rising to take the humongous thing from his driver. "That's all, Lewis, I'll drive Mrs. McKenzie home with me."

"Very good, Mr. McKenzie," Lewis said and left the room.

"So what did you bring?"

"I hate to admit this, since the whole fate of our relationship seems to rest on the contents of that basket, but I didn't ask."

Really?

Ethan stifled another smile. "Let's look for ourselves, then."

To Ethan's delight the scent of fried chicken came out of the basket when he opened one side of the lid. Still warm, the odor of the delicious food seeped into the room.

"They must be geniuses or something," Savannah said, gaping in awe at the contents before her. "There's even an apple pie in there."

"With enough money you can do just about anything."

"So I see," she said, but without a bit of fear or loathing. Her tone sounded more awe inspired.

Ethan took the cloth from the basket and spread it on the coffee table in front of the leather sofa in the corner of the room. "I hope you weren't planning to sit on the floor."

"Nope," she said, and happily joined him, sitting beside him.

Carefully removing the contents of the basket, Ethan covertly watched her. She wasn't angry with him, afraid of him, or arguing with him or his wealth. She had brought him food.

"I suppose you guessed that I've come here to apologize."

"Yep."

"Because I am sorry."

He peeked at her. "I know you are."

"I would never officially doubt you, per se, it's just that…"

He caught her hand so she would look at him. "I know. It's a very unusual situation, made even more difficult by my unusual life. I seem to have power and authority that I really don't have. No one does."

"For someone who doesn't have power and authority your staff certainly snaps to attention."

"They're paid to. The rest of the world is not. I'm not all that special or that hard to understand. If you stay with me long enough you're going to discover I'm perfectly normal."

He hadn't meant to imply that being perfectly normal also meant he had perfectly normal sexual appetites, but that seemed to be the thought hanging between them. Not just because that was the unresolved issue from their discussion on Monday night, but because he was holding her hand and looking into her eyes, and whether they wanted it to be or not their obvious sexual attraction was not something they could change or avoid.

But to his surprise she didn't look away. In accepting everything else about him and his life, it seemed Savannah was accepting that, too.

Not wanting to push her, and deciding to be content with even that small concession, Ethan dropped her hand. "We should eat this before it gets cold."

"Good idea."

She said it casually, but confidently and again Ethan's spirits lifted. She really was getting used to this. Getting used to him. Though he didn't want to push her, he knew he couldn't drag his feet, either.

"You know, Savannah, I still believe we could make this work for real. We like each other. We're going to have a child together. And we seem to be able to work through our difficulties."

She shrugged.

Not convinced she understood him, he added, "I think that means we would have a good relationship."

Savannah smiled. "Actually, Ethan, I don't want to get into this right now."

"Okay," he agreed because they were talking civilly again and he didn't want to ruin that any more than she did.

Obviously changing the subject, Savannah said, "It almost feels odd not having Josh here."

''Since he hooked up with Olivia, he doesn't work weekends anymore.''

Savannah turned to face him. ''I sort of guessed that.''

''Yeah. He's a very different man from the one you probably remember... Did you know he had a fiancée who died?''

''No.''

''She was his boss in New York. He took her death very hard. That's why he was so quiet here.''

''I can understand that.''

Ethan leaned back on the sofa, studying her as she picked at her chicken and remembering that her parents had died and what she had told him about her depression. ''I'm sure you can,'' he said, then dropped the subject because it was painful for her. ''After he and Olivia started dating he became more open and told me about her one night when he was working late...and he didn't want to be.''

At that, Savannah laughed. ''If he's as in love with Olivia as he appears to be, I see why.''

She looked around his office again, and, watching her, Ethan said nothing. Without warning or explanation she set down her plate and rose to pace.

''There's so much about this place that is the same, yet I feel so different.''

''You are different.''

''The last time I was here...in this office,'' she specified walking around the room, running her fingers over his books and mementos, ''you and I were talking about my parents' estate.''

''You were coming to the conclusion that you were going to have to move north.''

''And you were in the process of getting divorced.''

''Yes. I was.''

"Wow."

"Yeah," he agreed, nodding as he continued to watch her. "A lot has changed. You've been through a great deal," he added making sure she knew that he didn't take her life as casually as she seemed to think he did. "I wanted to tell you Monday that I really understood what you were explaining but you didn't give me the chance."

"And then you got mad."

He shrugged. "And then I got mad. But I still should have told you that I appreciated that your life hasn't been easy for the past two years."

"Those friends you met in Thurmont pulled me through."

Ethan chuckled. "I don't doubt it."

"No, really," Savannah said, turning to him with a smile. "I don't know what I would have done without them."

"They're good friends, Savannah. But you'll make other friends."

She shook her head. "I would love some more friends, but I don't want to have to lose the friends I have to make new ones. There's a part of me that feels the day will come when I'm going to need to return the favor of what Andi, Mandi, Becki and Lindsay have done for me."

"Friends don't hold accounts over your head."

"Oh, they wouldn't but I would. You see," she said, pacing around the room again, "one of the reasons they can so easily take over the bed-and-breakfast is that they helped me get settled in."

"After your parents died?"

She nodded. "I was lost. Mandi and Becki came over with a casserole or something to make friends, saw that I was floundering and the next day they brought Andi and Lindsay. And mops and brooms and three cookbooks. Basically, they taught me how to bake. Between the five of us we figured out a cleaning schedule that kept the bed-and-breakfast spotless and could still be handled by one person. They listened when I cried. They called my brother to get him to visit. They took me out to dinner and the movies because I couldn't seem to gather the spirit and enthusiasm to come up with the idea myself.''

"I see.''

She faced him. "Do you?"

Ethan nodded. Though he didn't want to, he did see. She was telling him that she hadn't made the choice to give up those friends. And if they made this a marriage for real, if she rolled the dice on a relationship they didn't even know would work, she would be turning her back on the relationships she had that she knew did work.

If he insisted she keep this marriage, she would permanently move away from all the friends who had come to mean so much to her. And he couldn't even guarantee that their marriage would work. He couldn't guarantee he wouldn't hurt her. As well intentioned as he genuinely was right now, he couldn't guarantee that he wouldn't break her heart, and the price would be her friends.

Never before had he realized how selfish love could be, but he was starting to see now. In fact, looking into her pale-green eyes, seeing the pain thinly veiled by desperate hope, he was beginning to feel guilty that he took her away at all.

Chapter Six

Ethan knew Hilton Martin had a penchant for white, but he never realized how much until he and Savannah entered his home the night of their wedding reception and the entire downstairs was bathed in white roses.

Delicate buds lined the stairway and sat in huge groupings in the open foyer, hiding the Italian marble and overpowering the crystal chandelier. They surrounded the sofa in the white living room to the right, and in the reception room to the left, which was the gathering point for people at most of Hilton's parties, pyramids of flowers seemed to take up every inch of space.

Savannah gasped, "Oh, this is beautiful!" at the same time that Ethan said, "Where are the guests supposed to stand?"

Gina laughed. She was dressed in an iridescent blue gown, and her sable hair was styled so that some of it was swept up into a knot while the rest tumbled down like a waterfall. She looked like the perfect hostess her father had trained her to be. "There are plenty of spaces between and around the pyramids of flowers. Besides, most of the party will take place in the tent outside." She cast Ethan a confused look. "I thought guiding people to the tents through the sea of roses would be romantic. Particularly since they are Savannah's favorite flower."

"I know," he said, because he did. Thank God. He remembered that from the one time in their shared past when she had gotten flowers from an admirer. But he saw the evidence again in Savannah's glowing face as she glanced around.

"They're just so beautiful," she said, looking like she would weep. Tears pooled in her eyes and, as always, Ethan's chest tightened.

"Yes, they are. And since you like roses so much, we'll have the gardener plant them anywhere you want," he said, jumping to her rescue by diverting her attention because he didn't want her to cry. Ever. About anything. He couldn't handle it.

She brightened immediately. "Really?"

"Sure," he said, thrilled that the simplest things made her happy. "We'll call Frank on Monday."

"There you are," Hilton said, interrupting Ethan as he stepped into the foyer, bringing Ethan's parents with him. Tall and dressed in a tuxedo, with his white hair combed off his face, he looked like the southern gentleman that he was. He embraced Savannah. "Hello, Savannah."

"Hello, Mr. Martin."

"No more of that," Hilton said with a laugh. "From now on I'm just plain Hilton."

"Okay," she said, but she laughed lightly, airily. "Hilton."

The second he released her, Ethan's father hugged her, and the second he released her, Ethan's mother took her turn.

"You look fabulous!" Penny said, then pushed Savannah away slightly for a closer inspection.

Ethan held his breath. The front of Savannah's hair had been braided in rows to pull it off her face, but the back hung in long loose curls entwined with something shimmering that reminded him of glitter. She had chosen a simple pale orange dress that fit to perfection at the round neck and cap sleeves, but gently expanded to hide her pregnancy without being obvious. The dress wasn't cool and sophisticated like Gina's spaghetti-strap creation with the dramatic drape of material that clung to her shoulders and cascaded down her bare back. Or expensive and elaborate like his mother's red silk gown. Savannah's dress was youthful and innocent. In a way, Ethan supposed, it reminded him of something a princess would wear.

His mother nodded her approval. "With all that beautiful red hair, peach is the perfect color for you."

Savannah grimaced. "You don't think I should have worn white."

"Whatever for?" Penny asked, then led Savannah into the living room.

Savannah laughed. "I don't know."

"Then it's something we won't worry about. Sit...while you can," Penny said, easing Savannah down to the sofa and taking the seat beside her. "Gina, do we have water somewhere for Savannah?"

"It's all arranged. The staff has been informed to watch her. If she looks tired, they bring her a chair. If she looks thirsty, they bring her water..."

Savannah gaped at Gina. "Really?"

Ethan chuckled. "Honey, you're the guest of honor. Nobody wants you to faint."

"Oh."

"Okay, so here's the plan," Penny said, taking Savannah's hands so she could have her attention. Dutifully, Savannah focused on his mother as she explained who would be attending this reception and gave a brief rundown on how Savannah should greet everyone.

Remembering his ex-wife's reaction to his mother's "helpful hints," which Lisa described as meddling, Ethan stiffened, expecting to have to referee an argument. But rather than be put off, as Lisa had been, Savannah took note of everything his mother said and even asked questions.

Ethan relaxed. "I'll be right beside her in the receiving line, Mother," he said, but he laughed.

"And I'll be right beside you. But Savannah doesn't want us correcting her in the line or even offering too many suggestions. This is all she needs to know. She'll be fine without us now. In fact," she said, giving Savannah a conspiratorial wink, "she may not need us anymore."

"Not hardly," Savannah said, but as the words came out of her mouth, the doorbell rang.

"That'll be Senator Johnson," Hilton said, straightening away from the doorjamb where he had been resting as he watched Penny brief Savannah. "Idiot likes to be the first person at every party."

"Savannah, Ethan, are you ready?"

"As ready as we'll ever be," Savannah said. Before she could hoist herself off the sofa, Ethan offered his hand and she smiled at him.

Ethan liked the fact that she would accept his help. He also appreciated the way she answered for them as if they were a team—because they were again. Though it appeared they had bonded in Thurmont, it had taken two clear-the-air conversations to solve the challenges posed

by his life in Atlanta. But he no longer had the feeling
that they were fighting each other, or even that they were
two sides of an issue forced together. Just as they stood
together the night he confronted her friends, they were
standing together now.

When they took their positions in the main room as
Hilton and Gina instructed, Ethan raised Savannah's hand
to his lips and kissed it lightly. This final seal of the
commitment cheered him and he knew from here on
every day would get easier. In fact, with the problem
under control the charade no longer seemed like an effort
to correct a mistake. Instead, what Ethan suddenly felt
was that he was getting a great gift.

"Senator Johnson," Hilton said, as the senator entered
the rose-filled room and met the reception line. "How
nice to see you." He made the quick introduction of the
bride and groom, though Ethan already knew the man
through his father, and then shuffled the senator on down
the line to his parents, as other people began to arrive.

Savannah took to the process as though she were born
to it and again Ethan marveled at her poise for someone
supposedly unsophisticated. She didn't falter or even look
tired throughout the admission of two hundred and fifty
guests, all friends and family of Parker and Penny
McKenzie.

At dinner, Ethan felt a stab of remorse about that. Her
friends had been invited to the actual wedding, but only
Ethan's friends and family were here now. Of course, he
didn't think the quartet watching her bed-and-breakfast
could make the eight-hour trip and Savannah didn't have
much family. Her brother hadn't been in touch with anyone in the past month and though Savannah knew he was
safe because he had detailed a very clear plan to her in
his final phone call, Ethan realized she wanted to tell him

to come home. The few aunts, uncles and cousins she had were scattered all over the United States and Savannah didn't really know them well. And her parents were dead.

Watching her happily converse through dinner, Ethan experienced compelling emotions, almost as if a thought or conclusion was trying unsuccessfully to register in his mind. The only one of the feelings he could really name was the protective instinct he had for Savannah because he understood it. She was, after all, carrying his child. But the other things completely baffled him. One second he felt respect and admiration for her toughness and her spirit, and the next he felt sort of warm and fuzzy—appreciative of everything she was doing for him, but in a different way, a way that went beyond simple gratitude.

Rising, Gina tapped her fork against a crystal goblet to get everyone's attention, bringing Ethan out of his puzzling reverie.

"You know," she said, glancing down the five long rows of tables set up under an elaborate, air-conditioned tent behind Hilton's house. "We never have seen Ethan kiss the bride, and I've heard stories about the actual wedding kiss that would curl your hair."

Ethan glanced over and saw Savannah blush prettily. Part of him experienced a wave of panic, thinking he should try to come up with a way to get out of this. Particularly since they already had a searing kiss they had to live up to. The other part knew that it would look odd if he balked at kissing his bride, and also that Savannah had to get accustomed to this. She knew that for the next few months they were supposed to be pretending to be in love.

He also recognized she understood and accepted that, when she turned to him with a smile.

Another smile.

She never once gave him a displeased or warning look. Not even during their arguments and disagreements. No matter how odd, awkward or uncomfortable the situation, she always smiled at him. The warm, fuzzy sensation enveloped his chest again, almost making it hard to breathe.

Holding her gaze, he offered his hand for her to stand. Though she was now six months pregnant, she rose gracefully, again reminding him of a princess. With one easy tug on her hand, he brought her to him, and bent his head and kissed her.

And just like the first time, the initial brush of her lips against his caused every ounce of common sense and reason to fall out of his brain and pure instinct to take over. His mouth opened, hers responded. Their tongues twined wetly. White-hot lava oozed through his veins, obliterating any remaining vestiges of propriety. With his hands on her shoulders, he inched her closer and she didn't fight or protest, but came willingly. He felt the raw silk of her dress under his palm and wished it was her bare skin.

Unfortunately, the image that brought to mind kicked in even more powerful instincts than those of protection and appreciation. What he wanted was to make love to her. He wanted it so much and so badly, his body reacted as if it would happen right then and there. It was that reality that brought him back to earth. He couldn't walk around a party fully aroused.

He eased back and Savannah gazed up at him. Instinctively, his hand went to her cheek. He couldn't believe that the entire time she worked for him he had missed how beautiful she was, how soft her skin was, how expressive her eyes were.

"Okay, I think they lived up to that kiss we all heard about," Gina said with a laugh, bringing Ethan back to reality.

He caught Savannah's hand and turned her toward their guests again. "That's the last kiss you get to see," he said, accenting the "see," and only half teasing. He didn't think his body would survive another, unless it was out of the line of vision of prying eyes.

The guests laughed. Savannah blushed and the entire party went back to normal.

Except for Ethan, who couldn't stop watching Savannah any more than he could stop himself from drawing the natural conclusions he drew. His parents adored her, and Savannah reciprocated the feeling, laughing with them for the ever-present photographer, which she didn't resent the way Lisa had. She teased his cousins. She danced with the six-year-old daughter of a friend. Though she always argued that she didn't fit in to his life, from what he was seeing tonight it was very clear that she did. Not because she was born and bred to this lifestyle, but because she wasn't. Bright and sunny, she was like a breath of fresh air to his stuffy family—his stuffy life. She made him happy. She made his life easier. And she was giving him a child.

In Ethan's mind it was clear that this wasn't an accident of fate. He genuinely believed he and Savannah were meant to be together. Permanently. Not only did she fit in to his life, though she claimed she didn't, but also she was very happy doing it. She was happier tonight than Ethan had ever seen her.

She didn't merely make him happy. He made her happy, too.

The simple truth was so intense for Ethan that he gave a quick excuse to Savannah and stole away for a few private minutes in Hilton's den. They were meant to be together. It was obvious. At least to him. The problem was he wasn't sure he could convince Savannah. She had some very compelling, very valid arguments for why she didn't want to stay married to him.

Running his hands down his face, he flopped down on Hilton's tall-backed leather chair and spun it toward the French doors. Closed blinds kept him from seeing what was beyond the glass, and he stared at them blankly.

"So, married again?"

Ethan turned to see Shane Thomas grinning at him. Tall and wiry, his blond cousin stood in the open doorway. Though Ethan had hoped for a few minutes of privacy to think this through, if there was anyone on this planet with whom he could be honest and maybe reevaluate this situation before he did something foolish, it was Shane. "I'll bet you're surprised."

"Let's just say I wasn't surprised to hear Savannah was pregnant. I knew only an act of God would get you to the altar again."

"Actually, Shane, it wasn't an act of God. It was a theft."

Shane laughed, but eased into the room. "What?"

"Close the door."

Obviously intrigued, Shane complied. "I have a feeling this is good."

"It's not merely good," Ethan said, serious, quiet. "It's the most confidential thing you will ever hear in your life, so if you're not willing to be sworn to secrecy, then I'm not saying another word."

Shane became serious, too. "Ethan, I never told anyone about the time we sneaked off to Europe when we were supposed to be at Kamp Wintamucka."

"That's Kamp Winnimucki," Ethan countered grinning.

Shane laughed. "What the hell did our parents see in that place?"

"I don't know. Maybe they thought all sixteen-year-olds liked mud."

"Whatever," Shane said, suddenly serious again. "What's the deal here, Ethan?"

"The bottom line is that Savannah went to a sperm bank to get pregnant because she was ready to have a child, and she wasn't in a committed relationship."

Shane's eyebrows rose.

"Lots of women do it. But in Savannah's situation, though she didn't really want to know the father, per se, she was very concerned about a nameless, faceless donor...."

"So you volunteered?"

Ethan shook his head. "No. Her brother was an employee of the clinic and he discovered I had a private sample stored there from a few years ago when Lisa was telling me she never wanted children. I hadn't touched it in so long, he assumed I had forgotten it, which I had. And he forged my signature so that they could use my sperm."

For several seconds Shane only stared in disbelief, then he whispered, "Good God, Ethan, I can't even begin to say what the papers would make of this."

"That's why it's all a secret."

"You married her instead of sending her to jail?"

"She didn't know what her brother had done. She had been my paralegal for two years when her parents died, and then she moved away. Her brother recognized my name because I handled the estate paperwork for them.

She wanted assurance that her baby's father was a decent man. Her brother provided it.''

"And you married her?" Shane asked again, still sounding confused.

"Sam Ringer is going after the party's nomination to run for president. Because he knows two big names are better than one, he's not waiting to announce that he's asking Dad to run for vice president on his ticket. He's doing it before the primaries...right about the time our baby is born. I couldn't risk this story getting in to the papers. I couldn't risk someone digging up the news that I was paying child support for an illegitimate child. It was all too much of a scandal.''

"Okay," Shane said, slumping on his chair as if confused. "But are you sure this was the right way to go?"

"I like her," Ethan said, wincing at the understatement. "I mean, even when she worked for me, I liked her. I understand her wanting a child, wanting to make a family for herself, because of both of her parents dying. I also know I can trust her...right off the bat I told her about my father running for vice president. My natural instinct has always been to trust her and I'm convinced getting married was the right thing to do.''

"But..." Shane perceptively prodded.

"But things are getting weird. She's perfect. She's wonderful. I would give half my portfolio to sleep with her.''

Shane laughed. "Oh, this is fabulous. Fifty percent of the women in this country want to sleep with you, and the one woman you want doesn't want you!"

Ethan caught Shane's gaze. "I didn't say that."

"Oh." Shane thought for a second, then said, "Then what's the problem?"

"There isn't a problem. I want to keep her and I'm going to."

"Just like a pet?"

"Not like a pet!" Ethan said and bounced from Hilton's chair to pace. "She doesn't have a family. She created this baby to get a family. Married to me she has family. My mother, my dad, my idiot cousins."

"That's good."

"Except she thinks her friends back in Thurmont are her family, and if she stays married to me she will lose them."

"But friends go in and out of your life, Ethan. You and I know that. You can easily make the case that real family like you're giving her lasts forever, while her friends will be leaving as soon as they find their own mate, their own destiny."

Ethan spun around. "That's exactly what I thought!"

"So you love her?"

Ethan shook his head. "I'm not going to make that mistake again."

"Oh, so this is more like a used car thing. You found one you like, you're committed to keeping it, and you don't have to risk real love because fate has taken care of getting you married." Shane caught Ethan's gaze. "That's a sweetheart of a deal. Everything you want. None of the risk."

"It's not like that."

"Do you love her?"

Ethan scowled. "I don't need to love her."

"So you don't."

"I don't want to be in love. I don't need to be in love. What Savannah and I have is perfect. We respect each other. We like each other. We're going to have a child. Love only gets in the way. I don't want it."

* * *

When Savannah felt the hand on her shoulder, she jumped and almost screamed. Instead, she put her palm to her chest and turned to find Penny McKenzie smiling at her.

"What are you doing, dear?"

"I came in to find Ethan, but he's talking with someone. I don't want to interrupt." She didn't mention that she had heard so much of the conversation that she couldn't interrupt. She wasn't sure she could face Ethan right now because everything she had been assuming tonight was wrong. Though she fought hard against it, and though it was absolutely the worst thing to do, Savannah realized she was falling in love with him. She had thought Ethan was feeling it, too. But he wasn't falling in love. Just as his cousin suggested, he was choosing to keep her the same way, and maybe even for the same reasons, someone chose a car, or a house, or anything that was necessary and convenient. But not something about which he was passionate.

Though she didn't want them to, tears sprang to her eyes. She blinked them back and smiled at her mother-in-law. "Let's just go outside without him. I'm sure he'll be along in a minute."

Penny studied Savannah's face. "Are you upset because he left you alone?"

"No. No!" Savannah hastily assured her. "I'm fine. I just, well, I just wanted to see him."

Penny's expression became warm and concerned. "It's very nice for a mother to see that the woman her son married loves him." She put her arm around Savannah's shoulder. "Do you know that?"

Savannah smiled. "I can understand that it would be."

"But it sort of hurts me to suspect that you don't really

The Silhouette Reader Service™ — Here's how it works:

If offer card is missing write to: Silhouette Reader Service, 3010 Walden Ave., P.O. Box 1867, Buffalo NY 14240-1867

NO POSTAGE
NECESSARY
IF MAILED
IN THE
UNITED STATES

BUSINESS REPLY MAIL
FIRST-CLASS MAIL   PERMIT NO. 7-7-003   BUFFALO NY

POSTAGE WILL BE PAID BY ADDRESSEE

SILHOUETTE READER SERVICE
3010 WALDEN AVE
PO BOX 1867
BUFFALO NY 14240-9952

Play The *Lucky Hearts* Game

and get...
FREE BOOKS & a FREE GIFT...
YOURS to KEEP!

Scratch Here!
then look below to see
what your cards get you...

Yes! I have scratched off the silver card.
Please send me my **2 FREE BOOKS**
and **FREE GIFT**. I understand that I am under
no obligation to purchase any books as
explained on the back of this card.

315 SDL DH4C　　　　　　　　　　　　　**215 SDL DH4A**

NAME　　　　　　　　(PLEASE PRINT CLEARLY)

ADDRESS

APT.#　　　　　　　　CITY

STATE/PROV.　　　　　　　　　　ZIP/POSTAL CODE

Twenty-one gets you
2 FREE BOOKS and
a **FREE GIFT!**

Twenty gets you
2 FREE BOOKS!

Nineteen gets you
1 FREE BOOK!

TRY AGAIN!

Offer limited to one per household and not valid to current
Silhouette Romance® subscribers. All orders subject to approval.

Visit us online at

www.eHarlequin.com

trust Ethan's love for you." She caught Savannah's gaze. "I can see in your expression sometimes that he surprises you when he does nice things. I also see you looking at him as if you want more from him. He may miss the signs, but I don't—" She paused, then added, "Do you want to talk about it?"

"I don't think that would be appropriate."

"Okay, then let me do all the talking. If I were in your shoes," she said, leading Savannah down the quiet hall to the back door so they could rejoin the party. "I would probably be afraid Ethan only married me because I was pregnant."

Savannah swallowed, but not at liberty to reveal anything she said nothing. She didn't even feel comfortable agreeing with Penny's assessment.

"That would make *me* feel insecure."

Realizing Penny wouldn't go on until she got some kind of confirmation, Savannah reluctantly nodded.

"And I would even venture to guess," Penny said, slowing the pace of her walk as if what she was about to say was of monumental importance, "that Ethan *is* holding something of himself back." They reached the end of the hall. Rather than push out into the night and the party, Penny stopped. "But the thing of it is, his first marriage—divorce actually—devastated him. His wife didn't want to have children. She was adamant, and Ethan shouldn't have married her, but he adored her. Unfortunately he is also the last McKenzie male. All those cousins you met, they're from my side of the family. When he and my husband die, that's the end of their line. Ethan was so confused," Penny said, holding Savannah's gaze. "That he went so far as to freeze sperm in a clinic. In case he died before Lisa changed her mind, he didn't

want to leave us without the possibility of a grandchild.''
She smiled wanly. ''An heir. A continuation of the line.''

''That's very sweet.''

''Ethan is a very sensitive man. That's why his wife
hurt him so much. She seemed as devoted to him as he
was to her, but one day she shocked us all by asking
Ethan for a divorce. Ethan was giving up everything for
her, but she changed her mind and filed for divorce. And
just as quickly as she asked for the divorce, she moved
to Oregon, got a job as a hospital administrator and no
one has heard from her since…except that her parents
continually remind Parker and me of how happy she is
without our son.''

''That's awful,'' Savannah whispered.

''It is, but it also should help you to understand why
Ethan is a little standoffish. If he's not quite as attentive
or loving as you might want in the beginning, Savannah,
give him time.'' She squeezed Savannah's hand. ''He'll
come around.''

Savannah licked her dry lips. ''Okay,'' she whispered,
knowing that in order to complete the charade she had
four or five months to live with Ethan so the promise
wasn't a false one.

Before Penny could say anything else, Ethan and
Shane came out of the den and Ethan waved to them.

''Wait for us.''

Penny turned to Savannah. ''Please. Don't do something foolish and don't be annoyed with him. Really, he
deserves a second chance.''

Savannah nodded but couldn't say anything because
Ethan and Shane made short order of the hall. Ethan immediately put his arm around Savannah's waist and
kissed her temple. Penny beamed, but Savannah's heart
sank. This was all part of an act designed to convince

Penny and though it was working, Savannah was the one who was getting caught up in the drama.

Or she had been until she heard Ethan's conversation. He didn't want to be in love. Those were almost his exact words. And that was the problem. He did not *want* to be in love. Because he didn't want to be in love, he wouldn't fall in love. If she was wishing for it, she and Penny were only out for heartbreak.

Chapter Seven

At eleven o'clock, Ethan and Savannah said their good-byes, thanked their hosts and walked out of Hilton's mansion to Ethan's Mercedes sedan, which Lewis had waiting in the circular driveway.

"Thank you, Lewis," Ethan said, handing Savannah into the back seat while the chauffeur held the door.

"You're welcome, sir," Lewis said, then got behind the steering wheel. Without waiting for instructions, he started the engine. When Ethan was comfortably seated beside Savannah, Lewis began to drive.

"You were wonderful," Ethan said, facing Savannah.

"Thanks. I needed to hear that. I was more than a little nervous."

"It didn't show."

"Good. I just went with the old adage and 'was myself.' It seemed to work out well."

"Yes, it did," Ethan said, but then he fell silent and Savannah was abundantly grateful. She turned her head to look out the window and watched the lights of Atlanta drift by.

It amazed her that she had kept up the facade all evening, but she had. And gracefully. However, now she was hungry and tired and she didn't want to play this game anymore. She just wanted to be left alone.

But she couldn't even find peace in silence. Every time she closed her eyes she remembered the things Ethan's mother had told her and her thoughts raced. She understood the pain of his divorce because she had seen most of it. Savannah had been sitting at her desk right outside Ethan's office door when the papers were served. She knew it had hurt him. She knew it had changed him. And she knew both of those things well, understood them well, because it had hurt her and changed her when Drew left her. It hurt her so much that she gave up on love, too. That's why she had created her baby the way she had.

But she didn't have a big family to fall back on for love and support the way Ethan did. She didn't even have the security of parents to depend on for unconditional love. She had no one. And having no one forced her to realize that a person could not live her entire life without love. Their baby would give her love. Their child would also return a sense of family to her. But nothing would replace the love of a spouse. Nothing. She might not have realized that until after the baby was conceived, and it might have even taken creating the child to cause her to see she needed grown up, companionable, sexual love in her life. But she knew it and she also knew she couldn't settle for anything less. Because she had nothing else. No one else.

Lewis maneuvered the sleek car onto the driveway in

front of Ethan's home. Ethan helped Savannah out of the car, said good night to Lewis and unlocked the front door.

"Is there anything I can do for you before we go to bed?" he asked casually.

"I'm kind of wound up and hungry," Savannah admitted, smiling sheepishly at him. "If you don't mind, I'm going to see if Mrs. Perez has anything in the kitchen to eat."

"Good, I'll help you."

Savannah's eyes grew round with distress. The last thing she wanted to do was spend more time with him. Not because he was difficult to be around, but because he was easy. Sweet. Nice. And being with him made her long for things she couldn't get from him.

"Oh, Ethan, I'm sorry, but I wasn't hinting for help and I also don't want help. I wouldn't be very good company anyway."

"Why don't you let me be the judge of that," he said, then he took her hand and led her down the hall toward the kitchen, and Savannah resigned herself to the inevitable. She wasn't going to keep her distance from this man. Not just because she was married to him, but also because he liked her. That much he had admitted. But it was because he liked her that this was so confusing. If he hated her, she could live the next few months out in complete solitude, pampered by his staff and off her feet, reading books and allowing Ethan into those parts of the pregnancy that interested him. Because he liked her, everything interested him. What she ate, how she slept, what she read. Up to now, he hadn't intruded, had given her privacy. But after what she had heard tonight and considering that he was leading her to the kitchen, she had to wonder if he wasn't going to start using his involvement to convince her they should make this marriage permanent.

"So are you having a craving?" he asked, flipping on the light to reveal the clean and shiny black-and-white room.

"No," Savannah said, but she laughed. "No craving. I'll just look around until something strikes my fancy."

"Okay. While you're doing that, I'll get out a bottle of sparkling grape juice. Tonight was such a success, I think we should toast it."

Savannah poked in the refrigerator for cold cuts, then went on a scavenger hunt for bread. From her peripheral vision, she saw Ethan retrieve a bottle of sparkling grape juice from a wine rack. He wasn't hovering, or monitoring what she put between her two slices of bread and Savannah wondered if her thinking hadn't gone overboard. Maybe he wasn't going to drive her crazy for the next few months. She hadn't heard the end of his discussion with Shane. For all she knew, his cousin might have talked him out of trying to keep her. She could be worrying for nothing.

She had just finished making her sandwich when he handed her the fluted glass. "Here's to a long successful relationship."

After sliding onto one of the tall stools by the counter, Savannah took the grape juice then clinked her glass to his. "Let's hope it's successful, because if it isn't that will mean our child isn't successful...which makes us bad parents."

"I think we're going to be wonderful parents."

Because Savannah couldn't deny that, she inclined her head in agreement, then sipped her juice. Cool and fruity it exploded on her tongue. "So do I."

"We're both intelligent, compassionate and in possession of a good sense of humor."

Alerted by a change in his tone, Savannah peeked across the counter at him. She couldn't tell from the expression on his face whether or not he intended to drag them down the conversational road of making this marriage permanent, but she wasn't biting because she did not want to talk about it.

"Are you trying to sell me something? Because you're starting to sound like an infomercial."

Ethan threw back his head and laughed with delight. "Yes. I guess in a way I am trying to sell you something."

Eyes narrowed, Savannah again studied him. If he was waiting for her to pick up that hint, he was going to be sorely disappointed. She wasn't going to bring up a subject she didn't want to discuss. "Well, forget it. I'm dead broke."

He shrugged, then leaned across the counter, laid his palm on her cheek and smiled into her eyes. "I'm not. That's the beauty of this, Savannah. We both have something the other wants."

Damn it! He was going to drag them down this road again. They had already been over this, and it infuriated her that he wouldn't even try to love her. Worse, she wasn't sure she could control her reactions. Now that she was over the hurt of what she had heard him say, now that she had had a chance to let realism and pragmatism do their work and bring her wishful thinking back to planet Earth, what she wanted to do was sock him.

But she knew she couldn't. She had to live with the man for another few months. Besides, he wasn't simply an obstinate male who didn't want to make a commitment. As his mother had explained, he didn't believe in love because his last wife had devastated him. In a certain sense, their experiences were similar. She didn't want to get hurt. He didn't want to get hurt. And they were protecting themselves. Unfortunately, they had decided on the exact opposite approach to do it. Still, she empathized with the fact that his divorce had been painful, and she didn't want to add to his misery by fighting with him.

So, she scooted away a fraction of an inch. Not enough to insult him, but just enough to pull herself out of his reach. She grabbed her sandwich to distract both of them from the conversation, then realized that with her own thoughts so clear it might be better to talk about it and hope this would be the last time.

"Ethan, I thought we agreed that this would be a strictly platonic marriage. In fact, I thought we agreed twice. Once when we made the deal and once when you tried to renegotiate it."

"Things changed again," he said and rounded the counter to sit on the stool beside her. "I'm not trying to scare you, Savannah. And I don't want to make you mad by bringing this up again." He paused long enough to catch her gaze, Savannah thought, to communicate with his expression that he meant every word of what he was saying. "But we do need to reopen this discussion because your big argument for not making this marriage permanent is that you don't fit in my life, and tonight you proved you did."

"I don't think so," she said and tried to shift away again, but there was only so far a person could go on a stool.

"Oh, I think we both know you did," he said, then chuckled softly, affectionately.

Syrupy warmth spiraled through Savannah and she knew this was the real reason she shouldn't have gotten into this discussion. Tonight, at their beautiful wedding reception, surrounded by the love of his family and friends, and believing all the PR created by Hilton Martin, she had accidentally taken a huge step toward falling in love with Ethan. If he didn't get away from her now, right this minute, even knowing he couldn't love her, she would take seven or eight new steps. She liked the way he looked. She *loved* the cool, masculine scent of him. She recognized his innate goodness. She had been on the receiving end of it so many times during the past few weeks that she understood giving and being kind was second nature to him. She liked his smile. She appreciated his sense of humor. And, dear God, she wanted to touch him. She loved when he kissed her. Melted when he touched her.

If he took this little game of his too much further, she would be head over heels in love with the man and then she might agree to something that was all wrong for her.

"I know what you're saying, Ethan, about fitting in," she said. "But my fitting in is not the only problem we have."

"Whatever the problem," he said, bracing one hand on the back of her stool behind her and leaning in as close as he could get. "I can solve it."

"No, you can't." She almost told him that she had overheard him say that he couldn't love again, which meant he couldn't solve the problem. But she didn't want to admit she had been eavesdropping. Worse, she didn't want to admit how much it hurt that he was so sure he couldn't love her.

"Why not?" he asked, leaning closer.

Savannah swallowed. "Just because."

"So far, Savannah, nothing you're saying is making

much sense." He shook his head, but inched closer. "You're losing the argument."

Without giving her a chance to respond, he presented the best argument of all. He kissed her. He pressed his smooth, warm lips to hers and every thought she had evaporated. Grasping her shoulders in his strong hands, he pulled her up, closer, until she was nestled against him, feeling his warmth, his strength, and the solidness of his masculinity.

And part of her begged. *Forget everything you heard. Forget everything you ever thought you needed. Please. Couldn't you focus on what you're getting, rather than what's missing?*

No.

She wished she could. With his warm mouth mating with hers and with his body close enough to touch, she definitely wished she could convince herself she could live without what was missing. But she couldn't. Because Drew hadn't loved her, the minute it was confirmed there was no baby in her womb, he left. And it crushed her. Devastation and pain resonated the whole way to her soul. She couldn't go through that again.

With a force she didn't know she possessed, Savannah pushed out of his hold. While he was still off balance, she struggled off the stool and away from him.

"I already told you that I don't think we should make this relationship permanent," she said, then remembered that she promised his mother she would give him a chance. But how? Every day it seemed she made another emotional promise or commitment, while Ethan skillfully avoided them. In fact, without a real commitment to love her, the only thing he was adding to the mix of their relationship was sex. They were already living together.

They were already friends. They already had a baby. The only thing they didn't do was sleep together.

Looking at her hands, rather than Ethan, Savannah said, "Whether you know it or not, Ethan, what you're actually asking from me tonight is to sleep with you because you've already got everything else from me. I'm here. I'm having your baby. But even if I wanted to make this relationship permanent, which I don't, I don't know you well enough to sleep with you. So back off."

He said, "Okay," quietly, calmly. So calmly, in fact, that Savannah looked up sharply.

"That I understand. Two years have gone by since we worked together, but even when we worked together we weren't involved in each other's lives. So, you're right. We don't know each other." He paused and smiled hopefully. "But you can't stop me from trying to fix that."

His words were a sweet promise, not a threat, but they didn't negate what Savannah had overheard. No matter how nice he was, he didn't want what she wanted, what she needed, and if she agreed to his proposition, he would break her heart.

Using one of his own tricks against him, she waited to catch his gaze before she said, "I might be a lot better at resisting you than you think."

With that she walked out of the room, up the stairs and to her bedroom.

The next morning she was awakened by a light knocking at her door. Confused, disoriented, she said, "Come in," before she fully had her bearings. Ethan entered carrying a tray with breakfast and a bud vase with one rose.

"Hi."

"Hi," she replied sleepily, glad she had chosen the most covering—and, coincidentally the most attractive—

sleepwear she had because even though she didn't want this marriage to become permanent, she didn't want to walk away with him thinking she was worthless, either. "What time is it?"

"It's after eleven."

"Oh, my gosh!"

"It's okay," Ethan said with a chuckle. "You don't have anywhere to go. But I was a little worried that you might be running low on fuel so I brought you breakfast," he added nodding down at the tray.

The consideration of it touched her and she avoided his gaze because she knew she would see the warmth and goodness in his eyes and something inside her would melt like it always did. "Thanks. I am starving."

"Like the rose?"

Still not looking at him, she surveyed the eggs and toast and hid her automatic smile. He sounded like a schoolboy trying to get approval from a favorite teacher. "Yes. I see you paid attention last night."

"At first that was because I knew I needed to know everything I could to keep the charade going."

"Now?" Savannah asked, biting into her toast, though she was pretty sure she knew the answer.

"Now, I plan on using every piece of information I have at my disposal to make you happy so that eventually I can seduce you and convince you to stay with me forever."

The pure honesty of it made her laugh. "Dream on."

"Oh, I will," he said and sat on the bed as she reached for her glass of juice. "I had some wonderful dreams last night," he said wickedly. "Want to hear them?"

She almost choked on her apple juice. "No."

"You might like them," he said in a suggestive, sing-song voice.

Savannah laughed again. He was the funniest, nicest man on the face of the earth. And probably one of the most sincere and honest. She wondered what kind of an idiot wife would throw away a guy like this and in the process hurt him so much that she ruined him for anybody else. Because even though he was saying all the right things, Savannah knew he didn't mean them in the way she needed for him to mean them. He would always like her, and maybe even love her. But he would never be in love with her. He would not take that last step.

Unexpectedly, the baby in her belly awakened with a stretch that expanded the pod around it. The sharp point of an elbow protruded with a pang of pain. Preoccupied with her thoughts of Ethan, Savannah wasn't prepared for the movement or the pain. "Ouch!" she yelped before she could stop herself.

Ethan bolted up on the bed. "What is it? What happened?"

"Your child just elbowed me."

He grinned. "Really?"

"Yeah," she said, grimacing. "If you look now," she said, pushing back the tray, then her covers and lifting the pink satin top of her pajamas, "you should be able to see it." She glanced at her tummy, saw the little triangle shape and pointed. "See."

"I see," he said, his voice soft and reverent.

"It's not a religious experience, Ethan," Savannah said, then she laughed, recognizing they needed to lighten the mood. "It feels like he's doing yoga. And though it might make him feel better right now," she said, grimacing again at the slight pain. "This does not feel good to me…. Damn I'm going to get heartburn."

"From him stretching?" Ethan asked with another grin.

"No, from bland toast and apple juice."

Ethan burst out laughing. "This is so incredible."

Savannah took pity on him and sighed in agreement. "I know."

"You live with it every day," Ethan said, catching her gaze. "It's upset your life, changed your body, given you heartburn," he added, then laughed like the devil as if he was amused at the oddness of the connection she had made for her discomfort. "But I only see this every once in a while."

Savannah chewed her bottom lip. This could be part of a ploy to seduce her. But in fairness she knew that even if it was, as the baby's father, Ethan had a right to be more involved in things than she had let him be to this point.

Without saying anything, she reached out and took his hand. Placing it on her tummy, she lifted her gaze to his and watched the wonder and awe that overcame him as he felt the fluttering movement beneath her skin. As if on cue, the baby shifted dramatically, and Ethan caught his breath.

"It's unbelievable."

"Yes, it is," Savannah agreed, except she was thinking again that it was unbelievable that a mean-spirited woman had tossed this wonderful man away. If she hadn't heard what she had heard the night before, she would be swooning at his feet right now. But she had heard. And just like he had a heart that had been broken and never repaired, if she let herself fall victim to the romance of this situation she might find herself in exactly the same position.

"Okay, breakfast is over," she said, smiling so Ethan wouldn't be insulted that she was kicking him out. "I need to shower."

He peered at her. "Then what?"

"Aren't we having dinner with your parents before they return to D.C.?"

He nodded.

"Then I would say I better call Gina for help shopping again because I don't have a thing to wear."

"I could come with you."

"No," she said, frowning. "I have a very limited budget and though I let you pay for last night's dress and even for the hair," she said, pulling a thick curl away from her head for emphasis, "there are some things I need to do on my own."

Even as Savannah said those words, she realized that was the truth. If she were smart she would stop letting Ethan blur the lines that separated their lives and get back to taking care of herself.

"So, I'm buying."

Giving her a curious look as if he thought she was crazy not to accept his money, Ethan asked, "You're sure?"

She nodded. "I'm sure."

Chapter Eight

Though Savannah knew she had to keep the lines between her life and Ethan's crystal clear, she also couldn't sit around and do nothing. Monday morning, roaming through Ethan's huge home, bored and desperate for something to do other than think about Ethan, she decided she would decorate his nursery. She knew he didn't have time, but more than that Ethan would have this baby for visitation. She had to accept that, and furnishing the nursery would be a physical acknowledgment of the fact. Plus, it assured her that while with him, her child would have everything he or she needed to be comfortable and happy.

Satisfied with that conclusion, Savannah called Gina to ask about department stores where she could begin shopping for the nursery. Excited to have been called upon for assistance, Gina didn't merely give Savannah names, she met her at the mall and shopped with her until two o'clock when she had interviews for executive assistants to replace Olivia.

Once started, however, Savannah couldn't seem to stop ambling from store to store, examining everything available. She wasn't ready to buy because she hadn't yet gotten Ethan's approval to spend his money. But she also wanted to choose what she genuinely wanted, not just what she could afford, because for the first time in her life money was no object.

She didn't let it bother her that Ethan's nursery would be fancier and prettier than anything she would provide for this baby, because when in Ethan's world the baby would always have more and prettier things. She satisfied herself with being happy to be part of the process.

Because she lost track of time, it was almost five when Savannah returned to Ethan's home. To her great surprise, he was already there and waiting for her. In fact, he was pacing the floor. When Lewis opened the front door to help her inside, Ethan rushed over as if she were injured instead of simply arriving home.

"Where have you been?"

Savannah looked at Lewis, expecting him to answer. But Lewis didn't say a word. He merely stood behind her, his arms laden with the clothes she had purchased to accommodate her expanding figure.

"Shopping," Savannah said, since Lewis said nothing.

"Are you okay?" Ethan asked anxiously.

Savannah laughed. "Ethan, I'm fine. I needed a few new things," she said, motioning toward Lewis, who stood silent as a big rock and held her packages as if they were weightless.

"Can we take these things upstairs?" she asked, not quite sure what the protocol was when confronted by an irate husband and responsible for a silent servant.

"Lewis, would you take those to Mrs. McKenzie's suite?"

"Yes, sir."

With that he left, and Savannah watched him go, knowing she would never get accustomed to this.

"Don't you worry that he'll tell someone we sleep in separate rooms?"

Ethan began to lead her into the living room. "Our rooms adjoin. Everybody thinks we sleep together, but have separate dressing areas."

"Okay. Whatever," Savannah said blithely, not about to argue with a situation that was designed to protect Ethan and which Ethan approved.

"So you were just shopping all afternoon?" Ethan asked quietly.

"Yes." Because she knew he had worried she wasn't concerned that he was questioning her until another thought struck her. "Why are *you* home?" she asked. Noticing that he was wearing jeans and a T-shirt, she added, "And how long have you been home? Aren't you guys supposed to be fighting some kind of hostile takeover attempt or something?"

He shrugged, lowered himself to the floral sofa and patted the seat beside him. "A takeover attempt would be if someone were buying up our stock, trying to get control of the company. But our stock's not public."

"Oh."

"What's happening," Ethan explained, laying his arm across the back of the couch—and by association Savannah's shoulders when she sat beside him, "is that a company called Bee-Great Groceries is beginning to build new stores in our territories. And Hilton's afraid we're going to lose our market share."

"Are you?" Savannah asked, comfortable sitting this close and talking so casually. She didn't agree with Ethan that she fit in to his world—even after weeks of living here she was having trouble getting accustomed to servants—but she did see that she could fit. She *would* fit, if they let this situation go on too long, because every day she learned something new and every day she got a little more relaxed.

In a sense that was the problem. She needed to be at ease and accepted in his world because as his child's mother she would always be a part of it. But she couldn't get *too* comfortable because it would make things more difficult for her every time she had to step back out.

He shook his head. "I don't know. I think it's inevitable that we lose market share in some places if only because of the law of averages. But Josh is a fairly smart cookie. We'll keep the bulk of what we have."

"In spite of the fact that he's preoccupied?" Savannah asked, arching an eyebrow in question.

Obviously catching the drift of what she was saying, Ethan laughed. "I think Olivia inspires him to new heights of creativity." He paused, tightened his arm around her shoulders affectionately, then asked, "So how was your day?"

"It was fine," Savannah replied, wishing she could melt into his arms because she was tired from shopping and it felt right and good to be comforted by him. But she reminded herself again that he didn't want to love her or anybody else and she needed love. If she accepted what he was offering she wouldn't merely get only half of what she needed, the rest of her life would be spent yearning for something she could never have.

Painfully aware of how lonely life could be without real love, Savannah rose from the sofa and paced away from him. "Actually, Ethan, there's something I want to ask you. I'm a little bored with nothing to do and I would like to decorate your nursery."

"That's a great idea." He studied her for a minute and though his tone hadn't hinted he was displeased, Savannah could see from the expression on his face he was unhappy that she had moved away from him. Because she knew he believed they should make this relationship permanent, she also suspected he might not be pleased that she had again divided their lives by pointing out that he would have his own nursery. The only thing she couldn't guess was whether or not he would address either.

Sighing, he ran his hand down his face, then said, "I want you to know that our baby is comfortable and happy when he or she is with me. Decorating the nursery will give you that assurance."

She almost breathed a sigh of relief, not just that he would let her decorate, but that he wasn't going to try to talk her into staying again. "Thanks."

"You're welcome."

Feeling he was as open as he would ever be, Savannah said, "I also think we should discuss visitation."

"I'm not ready to do that, yet." He rose from the sofa. "We've got plenty of time, Savannah. Right now the only decision we need to make is whether we want to go out for dinner or eat here."

"I'm too tired to go out."

"Good, I already asked Mrs. Perez to make pot roast. Hers is the best. You'll love it."

"You know, you've never let me cook for you."

"You don't have to ask," Ethan said, putting his arm around her shoulder and directing her to the spiral staircase in the foyer. "Any time you want to cook, you simply inform the staff so Mrs. Perez doesn't make dinner."

"Actually, since I get tired easily and with the nursery to keep me busy, I won't want to cook so much as bake."

"Then bake away," he said, guiding her up the steps. "But do it tomorrow. Right now, I thought you and I could make some decisions about the nursery. You know, color scheme, that kind of stuff."

"You care?" Savannah asked with a laugh.

"Let's just say I'm not putting a boy in a pink room or a room full of girlie ruffles and lambs."

"We can get a sonogram and find out the sex of the baby."

"Or we can do everything in rainbows so it doesn't matter."

Savannah inclined her head. "And ducks. Rabbits. Puppies. All those things are unisex."

"See how easily we compromise? We make a good team."

Savannah didn't comment on that because she finally realized why he was home early. He was spending time with her. That in and of itself wouldn't have been noteworthy, except Saturday night she had told him she couldn't make this a real marriage because she didn't know him, and now here he was spending time with her, getting to know her. That's why he hadn't disagreed about the nursery being "his." He hadn't accepted the fact that this relationship was temporary and in his mind the nursery belonged to both of them. But he was no longer arguing with words. If he intended to seduce her to his side he would do it with actions.

The thought almost took her breath, but before it could the opposite realization nudged at her. What if he had come home because he wanted to be there? What if spending time with her wasn't a tactic? What if being nice to her wasn't a strategy to get her to stay? She already knew he was a nice guy who wanted a child. Was it so far-fetched to think he simply enjoyed her company?

He opened the door to the empty nursery and Savannah glanced around. Two wide windows looked out over the rear gardens. At present, there were no curtains and the late afternoon sun poured in, hot and bright.

"If we're choosing pale colored curtains they will probably be light and airy, so we'll need blinds."

She stepped into the room and her feet sunk into thick white carpeting. "This might be a problem, too." She tapped her foot on the rug for emphasis. "I'm thinking a nice tile in here might be better."

"Whatever you want." He leaned against the doorjamb, as he also took a visual inventory of the room. "I can even have a contractor come in and change windows, knock out walls, add space…whatever. As long as everything isn't pink and girlie…unless, we have a girl…this is your call."

She turned to smile her thanks, but when she looked at him, her brain froze. Though he was smiling at her indulgently, as if enjoying her delight in having everything she wanted, exactly the way she wanted it, he was still the sexiest man alive. Tall and lean, with his shiny dark hair and compelling dark eyes, he was physically perfect to Savannah. Everything feminine inside her wanted to walk over, loop her arms around his neck and thank him with a kiss. She wanted to give him one of the devastating kisses he always gave her. She wanted to pleasure him the way she knew she could, if only because their chemistry was so strong.

He watched her as she studied him, and his dark eyes seemed to deepen in color. He stiffened against the frame of the door as if realizing what she was thinking, but resisted making the first move, because the decision was hers.

Savannah knew that was true and she recognized that

was another reason why he wasn't arguing her out of leaving anymore. He wanted the decision to stay to be hers. He had said his piece. She knew what he wanted. The choice was hers.

A current of electricity seemed to arc between them as they held each other's gaze. Everything about him was perfect. He was handsome, sweet, generous. He would give her anything and everything she wanted....

No, she amended in her thoughts, he would give her everything but the one thing she really wanted. His unconditional love. She couldn't accept him as he was. Unless he changed his mind about what he really wanted from this marriage, she couldn't accept his deal. She couldn't accept half, because it wasn't that she simply *wanted* unconditional love, she *needed* it.

The next morning, Ethan was at the breakfast table when she ambled downstairs after nine, still groggy though she had already showered and had dressed in jeans and a loose maternity T-shirt.

"You're going to get fired."

He folded the newspaper, set it aside and smiled at her. "I'm having my first baby. I'm sure Hilton understands."

Conceding that with a sigh, Savannah sat as Ethan pulled out her chair. "You don't have to pamper me."

"Maybe not for you, but I do for me."

"I know what you're doing."

He laughed. "Most generals do figure out the other's strategy. The trick is either outlasting your opponent or actually having the superior plan. You might know exactly what my plan is, but if my strategy is better than yours, I'm still going to win."

She scowled at him.

"You're not real chipper in the mornings, are you?"

"No."

"Then I think I will go in to work." He rose, summoned Mrs. Perez and instructed her to cook Savannah something special, then kissed Savannah's forehead and left.

The whole hell of it was, he had done it again. He saw she needed to be alone and he let her alone. Another man might have tried to cheer her up. Another man might have hung around attempting to be supportive. Ethan realized she didn't want to be cheered, didn't want support. She wanted food and peace. In that order. He not only recognized both, he gave them to her, because his entire goal in this situation seemed to be to give her everything she wanted so she couldn't bear to leave when the baby was born.

Damn the man was good.

Ethan came home from work early that afternoon and this time he brought flowers. The next morning, he waited for her to awaken before he left for work, and though her mood was better, again, he didn't smother her. He checked on her condition, made sure she would get a good breakfast, kissed her forehead and left. Then, at four o'clock that afternoon, which Savannah recognized had become his new arrival time, he appeared at her suite door, with fudge.

"Real fudge. I subcontracted it."

Savannah almost choked on her sugary treat. "How do you subcontract fudge?"

"Olivia's mother makes the best fudge. She started shipping a pound to Olivia every year for her birthday. I remembered it, thought you might like it and made a phone call."

"Oh, God, it's wonderful," Savannah said around a groan of appreciation.

"Good." He started walking toward her door, physically telling her he wasn't going to be a nuisance by hanging around pressuring her into staying.

She knew the plan, saw the pattern, but also knew she couldn't be so ill-mannered that she wasn't at least nice to him in appreciation for everything he did for her. "Anything you want to do for the two hours before we have dinner?"

He turned and shrugged. "Do you want to talk about the nursery again?"

"We could."

"Have you figured out what you want yet?"

"Yes," she said with a laugh. "And I don't think it's going to require a subcontractor."

"Paint?"

"Yes."

"There's your subcontractor," Ethan said, but he laughed, too. "Come on," he encouraged, opening his arm so she could slide under it. "We'll walk around the room, you can tell me what you want and I can make arrangements for painters, paper hangers and floor layers tomorrow."

"In that order."

"I'll let them decide the order."

Having a man admit he didn't know everything there was to know about subcontracting tickled her funny bone and Savannah laughed. She laughed again when he made fun of her color scheme of green, yellow and lilac. She laughed again when he lamented throwing out perfectly good carpeting because he sounded cheap and she knew he wasn't. And she laughed the entire time they were playing cards to while away the hours after dinner.

She laughed so much that she knew Ethan was winning in this little game-war of theirs. If he didn't stop being so nice to her she might give in if only because she recognized that if she could change her mind about this relationship, he could also change his. Maybe it was better to keep what they had, to hope it would grow, than to decide to give up without giving him a chance to change how he felt.

The only problem was, she had heard that conversation. She knew he didn't want to change how he felt, and if she stayed with him and gave him everything he desired, he would also have no reason to change.

At lunch the following day, she was so preoccupied with trying to decide what to do that Olivia noticed.

"What's up?" she asked, nudging Savannah's forearm to get her attention.

"Just tired," Savannah said with a sigh.

Though Olivia didn't argue, she frowned in a way that let Savannah know she wasn't convinced that being tired was the problem.

But if Olivia didn't believe her, Gina was doubly skeptical. "You know, Savannah, I wasn't born yesterday."

"Actually, you're the oldest," Olivia said, grinning before she shoved a forkful of salad into her mouth.

Gina shot Olivia an evil look. "That does it. Now I know you guys are hiding something from me because you brought up the one topic that always gets me to go off on a tangent. But it won't work this time."

Olivia only shrugged. Savannah said nothing.

"Come on, you two. I want to know what's going on," Gina said, not sounding angry, but frustrated. "There's a secret here. I can tell and everybody knows but me."

Olivia simply looked at Savannah.

"Gina," Savannah said, sighing heavily. "You're

right. There is a secret. And you are the only person in our circle who doesn't know. But there's a reason for that. Frankly, your father and Ethan believed if they could keep this from you, they could keep it from anybody."

Gina's eyes narrowed murderously. "Really?"

"Don't be mad," Savannah said, playing on her sympathies. "Ethan was only trying to protect my brother and his father."

"Spill it," Gina said simply.

"All right, I'm going to tell you, but I'm going to tell you for one good reason. I think I really need some advice."

"Hey, what am I, chopped liver?" Olivia asked indignantly.

"No, you're a woman so much in love she thinks everything is beautiful and good. When I tell this story, you're going to get dreamy eyes and give me bad advice...."

"Hey!"

"Hey, yourself," Gina said to Olivia, then leaned toward Savannah as if ready for the scoop. "You have my word that whatever your secret is, I will keep it. You also have my word that I will give you much better advice than your starry-eyed accomplice... Now, what's up?"

"It's a really long complicated story, but here's the Cliffs Notes synopsis. I got pregnant through in vitro fertilization."

Gina gasped. Although prepared for a secret, she obviously wasn't prepared for this one.

Ignoring her, Savannah continued. "I wanted a baby, but I was very skeptical about the process...especially picking the father. My brother worked at the clinic and he assured me that all the donors were physically healthy, smart, normal men, but I still had my doubts—however, I also still wanted a baby. I sort of pined for one. Anyway, one day my brother absolutely assured me he could get me a donor I would trust.''

"Oh-oh," Gina said, apparently figuring out where the story was headed. "I know that when Ethan and Lisa were married she didn't want to have kids and if this is going where I think this is going, I'm guessing that he froze sperm or something because he's an only child... Oh, good grief.''

"I think you have the long and short of it," Olivia said, pushing the story along, then patting Savannah's hand in support. "No sense dragging us through all the gory details.''

"Obviously, Ethan found out," Gina said.

Savannah nodded. "Getting married was just the clean way to handle things for his father and my brother.''

"But..." Gina prodded.

"But now Ethan wants to keep the marriage. He wants us to try this for real.''

"Ohhhhh!" Olivia cooed.

Savannah shot her a perturbed look. "See. She's starry-eyed and silly.''

"Actually, Savannah," Gina put in, biting her lower lip. "So are you. You like Ethan.''

"Gina, the truth is I could love the man. But he doesn't love me.''

"How do you know?''

"He's said it.''

Gina shrugged. "How does he know? He was in a miserable relationship for years. He wouldn't know love if it jumped up and bit him on the butt. He just needs time.''

"You think?" Savannah asked cautiously.

"Yeah, I think that's the real bottom line, and that's really what you're asking me," Gina said, reaching out to take Savannah's hand. "He's been a family friend for years. He had the worst marriage in recorded history."

Olivia seconded that. "Josh told me Ethan's wife, Lisa, was a spoiled southern belle."

Gina shook her head. "I'm a spoiled southern belle," she said, pointing at her own chest. "And, trust me, Lisa went beyond that. A real belle would never stoop to the levels of meanness this woman went to to get her own way. She doesn't have to."

"So you're saying there's hope?"

Gina laughed. "Oh, good gravy, yes!" She laughed again. "Oh, Savannah, you are the best thing that ever happened to that man. If you were to love him, just a little, he would come around."

"And if he doesn't?"

"He will," Olivia said confidently.

Savannah only looked at her.

"Well, he will," Olivia said. "Nobody thought Josh would ever be able to love again…."

"But this is different," Savannah said, being completely honest with her two friends. "Josh's circumstances were uncontrollable. His fiancée died. Ethan's wife was deliberately mean. She might have ruined him for life. If I decide to let myself fall in love with him, I could be setting myself up for a big fall."

"Then you better choose carefully," Gina said, and Olivia gaped at her. "What?" Gina asked, returning Olivia's odd look. "You think I'm being a skeptic?"

"Yeah," Olivia said.

"Well, maybe, just maybe," Gina said. "I think it's smarter to be careful than to jump into things that might get you hurt."

"Amen," Savannah agreed, because she knew she needed to protect her own heart. It occurred to her that Gina sounded like she was speaking from experience and she would have asked her what had happened, except Ethan walked into the restaurant and every thought Savannah had dropped out of her brain.

Not only could he take her breath away just by the way he looked, but there was an absolutely stunning blonde by his side.

Chapter Nine

Savannah turned to Gina. "Who is that?"

Gina followed the direction of Savannah's gaze, and her eyes widened with disbelief. "Great. Damn it."

"Who? What?" Olivia said, turning around and seeing Ethan and the blonde. "Oh."

"That's his girlfriend, isn't it?"

"Well, I wouldn't call her a girlfriend," Olivia said uneasily. "But she is the woman he was dating right before you guys called Josh and asked him to be your best man."

"Right. You wouldn't call that a girlfriend," Savannah said, trying to make herself too small for Ethan to see as he walked through the restaurant with the woman and was led to a table in the back of the room. "Well, I guess this makes my decision very easy," she said coolly, but inside her stomach had twisted in knots and tears desperately wanted to pool in her eyes. Stubbornly, she wouldn't let them.

Gina said, "Savannah, don't. I'm sure there's—"

"A good explanation?" Savannah asked, then cleared her throat because she refused to let this get to her. She knew the score going in. She was not in a real marriage. Ethan had confused her by trying to persuade her to make it a permanent marriage, but he never told her he loved her. He hadn't lied. He had been honest. He wanted them to stay together because it was convenient for him, not because he loved her. She was the one who had everything garbled in her brain. And if she looked at this objectively, seeing Ethan with another woman had simply cleared her muddled thoughts again. She should be thanking him.

"I'm sure there's a good explanation, too," she said calmly, trying to placate her friends. "Let's go while he's too busy getting seated to notice that I'm here."

Olivia and Gina exchanged a look, but neither said anything. Both rose silently and followed Savannah out of the restaurant. Because Lewis was waiting to drive her back home, they also didn't argue when she refused their company for the afternoon. She kissed their cheeks with a smile on her face and even made chipper small talk with Lewis during the thirty-minute trip to Ethan's home. She wouldn't let herself be upset. She *wouldn't*. Because she wasn't supposed to fall in love with him. And she wouldn't. Damn it! She wouldn't. She absolutely positively couldn't. And he had given her the ammo to save herself. Again, she reminded herself she should thank him and use that to keep herself happy through the afternoon.

But when Ethan came home at four, the hypocrisy of the situation shot fury through her. She wasn't so stupid that she didn't recognize that he was coming home early every day so they could get to know each other. He wanted to dilute her argument because he kept insisting they should make this union permanent. Yet, he had the gall to have lunch with another woman, at a restaurant where her friends could, and she *did*, see him!

How dare he!

When he stepped into the sitting room of her suite, she threw a pillow at him. "Get out."

"Hey!" he complained, tossing the pillow to the window seat. Adorned with a fat floral seat pad, white lace curtains and a thin blind the window was both pretty and functional, as was the rest of her comfortable sitting room. Green plants sat on the cherrywood accoutrements that accented the rose-and-mauve flowers in the print of the small sofa and chair. A burgundy rug sat on the polished hardwood floor.

"I had a hard day. You could be nicer to me."

"Ha! Nicer? To you? I don't think so."

"Is this one of those pregnancy things again?"

"You wish. Look, Ethan, I'm not one for beating around the bush and I abhor pretense."

The way she said abhor made his eyebrows rise. "You are really angry."

"Oh, and you wouldn't be, if I started seeing one of my old boyfriends while I was demanding that you play the role of loving husband for my father!"

Because she was half lying on the sofa, he sat on the rose-and-mauve chair by the window. "Now, you're confusing me."

She tossed her magazine onto the coffee table and it landed with a smack, ruffling the bright green leaves of the ivy vine. "I was at the restaurant with Gina and Olivia today. I saw you with the cool blonde."

"She's a colleague."

"Olivia told me she was your last girlfriend."

"She was," Ethan agreed casually because it was true.

"But when I decided to marry you, I gave up other girl-friends. That's the whole purpose of the little ceremony with the vows we went through." He kept his voice soft and calm, though inside anger began to bubble. This was a woman who kept him at arm's distance, refused half his gifts and was suspicious of everything he did. On days she felt like hell, he babied her. On her bad days, he made things better.

He didn't want to come home to accusations. He wanted a little spoiling himself. No. What he wanted was to lose himself in Savannah. He wanted to talk about the baby. Talk about her day. Hope against hope that she might come around to his way of thinking about their marriage. Instead, he got a pillow in the face.

"Ashley and I were taking care of my frozen sperm. If I... We..." Getting upset again, he pushed himself off the chair, stalked to her window and stared out at the garden. "Let's just say our baby might be my last child."

"Don't play on my sympathies."

"Don't make me any more irritated than I already am," Ethan warned, wondering where the hell sweet Savannah had gone and why she was so mad over a situation that could be easily explained. Every time he looked at her he saw his hope for a family, for a normal life. But if he couldn't get her to stay married to him, he knew he wouldn't have a family. He would have one child and he would only have that one child part-time.

Plus, his feelings for Savannah went beyond the baby and even beyond wanting more babies with her. She had brought unexpected hope into his life, and the ability to risk wishing for things he had once thought only existed in fairy tales. He wouldn't go so far as to say she made him believe in love again, but she had made him believe that a man and a woman could forge a bond, create a union strong enough to take them through the rest of their lives.

He knew the connection of the child started it, but it was more than that now. He wanted to kiss her and hold her and remember there were good things in life. To remember that there was a big difference between having sex and making love because he knew that with Savannah everything would be different.

He desperately wanted to feel that difference right now. This minute. Because he needed her.

"You know, you could leave if you don't want to be irritated by me anymore."

"Savannah, what I want right now is so far removed from what you're thinking it could be the polar opposite," he said, walking to the sofa on which she lay. "And," he added taking hold of her shoulders and turning her around so that she was facing him. "It's probably what you want least in the world."

He bent his head and kissed her. He thought she would resist, but she didn't. Her lips softened beneath his, then opened, and immediately the warmth of tender affection poured through him like very good, very fine wine, but he pulled away quickly before he was mesmerized or bewitched, because this time she wasn't winning. He wasn't going to let her get away with always pretending she didn't want him as much as he wanted her.

He gazed into her eyes and the soft vulnerability he saw in them told him several things. First, she wasn't really angry but confused. Try as she might she couldn't hide that she was getting feelings for him too…that was the reason she was mad at him. Not because she had seen him with another woman, but because seeing him with another woman forced her to admit she had feelings for him and she didn't want them.

Second, he could seduce her if he wanted. Right now. Because she did have those feelings. When they were close like this she wasn't any stronger than he was. Third, she wanted to be seduced. She wanted him to take her in his arms and kiss her until neither one of them could think. Then she wanted him to make love to her. But because she couldn't admit she wanted it, he couldn't do it. If he took her before she could admit this was what she wanted, then she would always have the open door to leave.

Besides, he didn't want a marriage based on passion. He wanted an honest relationship. No sweep of desire, but an agreement. A commitment. Honest. Dispassionate. Binding. He didn't want a commitment based on something so capricious as an emotion. He wanted it based on common sense, loyalty and friendship. If he could get that with her, then they didn't merely stand a chance, they would probably have a great relationship. If only because it would be honest.

No matter how much he wanted her, no matter how much she wanted him, if they couldn't have this relationship on the right terms, they couldn't have it at all.

He pulled away. "I'll send for you when dinner is ready."

The evening meal actually went much smoother than Savannah had anticipated, given that she knew Ethan was angry with her. His good breeding superseded any emotion and the conversation was cordial, even light at times. She found herself relaxing, then eating more than she should, then wanting to fall asleep on the sofa. With a laugh he guided her up to her room, asked if she wanted help getting into a nightgown, then left without another word when she told him she could manage on her own.

At breakfast the next morning, a visitor never would have guessed they had fought.

"It's the strangest thing," Savannah told Gina when she came to Ethan's home that afternoon to help measure the nursery. "He can turn off his moods like a water faucet."

"I think you have to be able to when you're in the public eye the way he is because of his parents."

"I suppose," Savannah agreed, walking the tape measure to the window, as Gina scribbled numbers.

"And you also have to take into consideration that his wife was hateful," Gina said, making note of the numbers on the tape. "Though he never showed it in public, I can guess that his wife made his life a living hell. I'm surprised he came out of the situation with his sanity."

"Um-hum," Savannah said as the phone rang. She let someone from the staff answer it, but wasn't surprised when Joni came upstairs and summoned her to let her know Ethan was calling. "I'll be back in a minute," she told Gina then scurried toward the door.

"Don't hurry on my account," Gina said with a laugh and Savannah almost cursed her stupidity, realizing Gina could see she was eager to talk with Ethan.

"Hey," she said, after picking up the receiver of the phone in her sitting room.

"Hey," Ethan replied. "Guess what?"

"What?"

"I hired someone to help with childbirth lessons."

Savannah's brow furrowed. "I'm not having natural childbirth, Ethan. I've heard about the pain. I know drugs are available. I would like to tell you I'm brave enough to try this on my own, but I'm not. I want the help of modern science."

Ethan laughed. "And you can have the help of modern

science, including the help of the guy who is going to come to the house tonight to teach us what to expect and how to handle it.''

''Oh.''

''Yeah, oh,'' Ethan said, laughing again. ''Who's the one of us who is thinking here?''

''You are,'' Savannah said, hearing the affection in her own voice because he was always thinking. He was a thoughtful, wonderful, unselfish man, and Savannah knew there was no help for it. No matter how hard she had tried to prevent it she was falling in love with him.

No, she already had fallen in love with him. That's why it was such a relief the night before that he wasn't angry with her. That's why she scurried out the door, eager to take his call. She was already in love with him. What she was doing right now was admitting it.

''So?'' Gina asked when Savannah walked into the nursery again.

''So, he's hired someone to come to the house tonight to teach us about labor and delivery and to teach us how to handle it.''

Gina shook her head in wonder. ''Sometimes he can be downright adorable.''

''I know,'' Savannah whispered, walking to the window.

''And you love him.''

Savannah squeezed her eyes shut. ''Yep.''

''Oh, Savannah, that's great.''

''No, it isn't. He doesn't love me. He cares about me. He even likes me a great deal and thinks I'm doing such a good job as his wife that he's asked me to consider taking the job permanently...''

Gina prodded. ''But?''

''But he doesn't love me. And I need for him to love

me. I don't want to spend my life worrying that another woman is going to come along, catch his eye and cause him to leave.''

"Ethan's not like that!" Gina gasped.

"He's also not in love."

"I would debate that," Gina said. "But even if we go with your theory that he doesn't love you, I would also say that he has every reason in the world to be a little standoffish. Then, I would add that a little help from you, a little patience, maybe even a little push," she said, nudging Savannah to make her laugh, "would bring him around."

"I don't know."

Gina put her hands on Savannah's shoulders and forced her to face her. "Listen to me. From everything you've told me, Ethan already does love you. Are you going to let him get away because it might take him a little longer than normal to realize you're not going to hurt him? And to realize that it's safe to admit he loves you?''

Savannah shook her head. "When you put it like that, it does sound silly."

"Of course it does," Gina said. "You mark my words. If you stay, a year from now you're going to thank me because Ethan's worth it."

That night when the child-care professional arrived in the den, Savannah saw the proof of what Gina said.

Floyd Brewer was young and enthusiastic, and took his job very seriously. About twenty pounds overweight for his short height, he nonetheless dressed in a trendy T-shirt, cargo shorts and sandals. His spiky light brown hair was streaked from the sun.

"Oh, the pillows are great!" he chirped, nearly skip-

ping into the den where oversize pillows with covers de-
picting bright cartoon characters—another gift from
Ethan—littered the leather couch. Savannah sat in the
midst of them. "And you must be the mother-to-be."

"I would be in desperate need of a diet if I weren't,"
Savannah laughed, looking down at her protruding
tummy.

"Aren't you adorable?" Floyd said, taking both of her
hands and then giving her a smacking kiss on the check.

"I like to think so," Ethan said as he leaned against
the doorjamb and crossed his arms on his chest as if he
were almighty annoyed that fun-loving Floyd had kissed
his woman.

Floyd laughed. "You damned well better," he said,
shaking his finger at Ethan. "Now," he said, flinging his
arms in dismissal as he looked around the room. "The
first thing we need to do is have a preliminary discussion
so that I understand how much of this process you already know."

"Not much," Savannah admitted as Floyd began shifting pillows to make room on the sofa. With a quick wave
of his fingers, he indicated that he wanted Ethan to join
Savannah, then he leaned against the huge mahogany
desk so that he was facing both of them.

"I understand your mother passed on," Floyd said
kindly.

Feeling tears spring to her eyes, Savannah nodded.
Ethan put his arm around her shoulders for support.

"As I explained, her mother was killed in an accident
a few years ago."

"And we all know mothers are the best source of information, especially about the first baby," Floyd continued, launching into a detailed explanation of what was
about to happen to Savannah.

For twenty minutes Floyd lectured them on pain and how to overcome it through focus. Savannah listened intently, but she also stole a few glances at Ethan, ostensibly to confirm that he was paying as much attention as she was. But she was really peeking at him because she was so impressed by how sweet he was and so confused by how he could be so sweet, yet couldn't take the final steps of commitment to a real relationship.

And she wondered if she wasn't splitting hairs.

"Now, we'll just do a few quick breathing exercises before I go tonight, but I also want you to know that your assignment for the week is to think of every question you might have." He paused and caught Savannah's gaze. "No question is stupid. No question is too personal."

"Maybe not for you," Savannah said with a laugh.

Good-natured Floyd laughed, too. "Honey," he said, then took her hands again. "Nine chances out of ten, after this baby is born you will never see me again in your life. It won't matter if I know the color of your underwear. All your secrets are safe with me."

Looking into his eyes, Savannah knew it was true. "Okay, I'll start a list tomorrow."

"Okay," Floyd said, clapping his hands together to indicate the closing of one subject and the opening of another. "Let's do those two breathing exercises just to give you the feeling that I've earned my money, then I'll be on my way."

To Savannah's surprise, Ethan laughed. After forty minutes of listening to Floyd try to make him laugh, Savannah finally got the pleasure of hearing him chuckle. She glanced at him.

He smiled. And everything inside of Savannah melted. He hadn't laughed until he was sure he trusted Floyd. But ultimately, he had trusted Floyd enough to smile.

Again, tears sprang to Savannah's eyes, but this time it was because she understood what Gina had been telling her. Somewhere inside his soul, Ethan knew he loved her. He *knew* it. He behaved as if he loved her. He simply couldn't say it. And she would be a fool to throw this away just because he needed time.

After twenty minutes of learning to say hee-hee-hee and who-who-who while lying on her back, her shoulders propped up by Ethan's knees and with a cartoon character pillow anywhere she wanted it, they finally said goodbye to happy Floyd who not only kissed Savannah's cheek, he also hugged Ethan.

"Are we going to be able to put up with that for another eight weeks?"

Savannah laughed with glee. "You picked him."

"No, I didn't," Ethan admitted, guiding Savannah to the stairway. "My paralegal, Mrs. Cronauer, chose him. I just interviewed him."

Savannah cast him a wry smile. "But you interviewed him."

"You bet I did."

She laughed. "Well, thank you. I appreciate it," she said, stopping at her suite door when they reached it. "My doctor had suggested I do something like this, but it didn't sink in why I would need to until I heard Floyd tonight."

"You're welcome."

An awkward silence settled over them. It wasn't really late, only about nine-thirty, but Savannah knew they both read before falling asleep and that was why they had climbed the steps rather than return to the living room.

With Ethan uncomfortably remaining outside her door, as if he didn't want to leave but couldn't find a reason to stay, everything she had talked about with Gina tiptoed through her brain. This was the right guy for her. This was the right marriage. She was also the right woman for Ethan, if only because she loved him. He also knew this was the right marriage. But he needed a push, more like an assurance from her that she was as committed as he wanted them both to be. And she knew exactly how to give him that assurance. All they had to do was consummate this marriage and the commitment would be made.

She licked her dry lips and peeked up at him. He was staring down at her as if he knew there was something on her mind, but didn't have a clue.

Heat and nerves rippled through her. She had never seduced a man before. Worse, so much rode on this seduction that it was doubly difficult. Gingerly walking her fingers up the buttons of his shirtfront, she held his gaze and said, "I have to shower before I go to sleep."

His eyes narrowed as if he were confused, and he said, "Okay."

Her fingers climbed a little higher, then stopped at the second button because the first button of his shirt was already open. Still, she held his gaze. "I think I would like for you to shower with me."

His peered at her as if he hadn't heard correctly. "What?"

"I've decided you're right, Ethan. We're married. We like each other. We want to make our commitment permanent. We both know the best way to do that." She paused and took a short breath for courage. "We both know the *only* way to do that."

He stared at her. "Are you sure?"

She didn't hesitate. "Yes."

As soon as she answered Ethan's question, Savannah turned, opened the door and revealed her quiet sitting room to him.

Ethan hovered by the door, but she didn't look back. She left the door open, expecting him to follow her. When she reached the center of the room, she faced him, her fingers immediately going to the top button of her blouse.

He almost ran inside the room to stop her. "No," he said, clasping her fingers to remove them from the button.

"No?" she asked, wide-eyed, frightened and so incredibly beautiful in her innocence that he almost shook with gratitude.

"If we're going to do this we're going to do this right," he said, then bent his head and kissed her.

Chapter Ten

At first his lips were warm and sweet, coaxing Savannah into relaxing because God knew she was tense. She had never seduced a man before, or made love when it was so important. She loved this man. He didn't think he could trust love. She had to prove to him that he could. She didn't necessarily feel that the outcome of this one event dictated the rest of their relationship, but she did know it was the turning point.

"Don't be afraid," he whispered against her mouth.

"I'm not." She paused. "Really."

"Really?" he asked, then chuckled and pushed away so he could see her face. His brown eyes were serious, concerned. "Savannah, is this what you truly want?"

"Yes," she said, because it was. She knew she loved him. She knew Gina was right. Somebody had to show him trust and love first, before he would take the risk again. As far as she was concerned, this was the initial step in that process.

Ethan didn't say another word. He scooped her off her

feet and carried her through her suite into his bedroom. Unlike her room that had splashes of pink and burgundy to accent the white walls and wooden floors, his room was dark with color. Navy blue curtains sat against forest green walls. A blue, mint green-and-beige print comforter held forest green pillows. Light pine kept the floor pale, except thick green rugs were scattered about. It was definitely a man's room and Savannah shivered realizing he had brought her to his domain to make a statement. If they did this, there would be no turning back. She would be his.

He set her on her feet and between quick kisses, he easily stripped off her blouse, then wrestled away his own shirt, revealing his chiseled chest which was covered with thick dark hair. Not giving herself time to think or panic, she kicked off her shoes and he followed suit. Then he kissed her again. With his hands on her waist, he pulled her closer. He sipped at her lips as if getting her accustomed to this second stage while at the same time going slowly enough that she could back out.

But she wasn't going to change her mind. Though he might have brought her to his room to make a point, the very fact that he would allow her into his personal space spoke volumes. It said he wanted her in his life—his private life—and that was a concession so close to love, Savannah's blood hummed through her veins.

His palms slowly slid from her waist to her shoulders and down again before he let them inch around her to examine the form housing their child. He smoothed his hands along the protrusion, caressing it, loving it. Then slowly, as if they had all the time in the world, he returned them to her back, kneading up the curve of her spine and down again.

Savannah felt real love radiating from his tender touch,

and when he reached for the clasp of her bra she wouldn't allow herself to stiffen with apprehension. Instead, she again forced herself to relax. He released her swollen breasts from their confines and slid the lacy garment down her arms, letting it fall to the floor, then he stepped back, far enough away that he could look at her.

"I can't believe how beautiful you are, and how lucky I am that you're here."

Carefully, reverently, he covered her breasts with his palms and as the warmth of his hands rippled through her, she smiled at him. "Actually, Ethan, I think I'm the lucky person."

He said, "Not hardly," before he kissed her again, pulling her so close that her breasts nestled against his rock-solid chest. This time when his hands slid down her back, he let them fall beneath the waistband of her jeans, taking advantage of the elasticity so that he could tug them down. When they were as far as they could go without real assistance, he stepped away and pulled them off.

"You're fabulous," he whispered.

"Yeah, well," she said, urgency coupling with a sliver of fear as she sat on the bed. "Now, I'm getting a little nervous."

"Okay," he said, as he divested himself of the rest of his clothes and joined her on the bed. Careful not to hurt her, he lay beside her, positioning them face-to-face. With his hand resting on her side, he kissed her the way he had the day of their wedding. Except this time their chemistry wasn't a surprise. This time, when his tongue slid into her mouth, she expected the explosion of desire, welcomed it, and welcomed the new invasion of arousal that coursed through her.

When he cupped her breast, moist heat enveloped her

and a new wonderful wantonness. With every minute that passed she felt more his and knew he was more hers. Her fingers itched to touch him, to feel the solidness of his flesh beneath her palms. Slowly, carefully, she slid her hand along his arm, to his shoulders, then lightly raked her fingers through the thick mat of dark hair on his chest. And it struck her that this was what making love was supposed to be. With gentle touches and exploratory caresses, they were committing to each other. She was telling him she would share the burdens and joys of his life. He was telling her he would share the burdens and joys of hers. And they were telling each other they would raise this baby together.

And that, she supposed, more than the flashes of heat and the shivery need, made making love with Ethan McKenzie the most memorable event of her life.

The next morning, Savannah awakened to both the warm rays of sunlight pouring in through the window across the room and the warm morning smile of the man she loved.

"Sleep well?"

"Better than I've ever slept," she admitted, snuggling against him, absorbing his warmth, enjoying being with him. Everything was perfect. He loved her. He might not be able to say it, but she knew it when he made love to her. They were having a baby. They were making the family both of them wanted. Nothing could be better.

He ran his hand along the curve of her torso, then caressed the mound of baby between them. "I hate to say this, but I have to go. I just wanted to make sure you were okay."

"I'm more than okay. I'm wonderful."

"Me, too." He smiled again but Savannah noticed that his smile didn't reach his eyes.

"Are you okay?"

"Yeah," Ethan said with a small laugh. He rolled over and sat up. "But I have to get going."

He rose from the bed, gloriously naked and Savannah couldn't take her eyes off him, marveling at how lucky she was. Their lives were joined. There was no question about that now. If Ethan was a little apprehensive, she accepted that, accepted him. It might be difficult for him to adjust but in her heart she knew he would.

He stepped into the bathroom at the same time that the phone on the bedside table rang. Realizing the staff would think her and Ethan asleep, and that this very well could be her brother, Savannah quickly reached for it. She hadn't heard from Barry since he left. Though she knew he was safe because he was an adult who had been on his own for years, she also recognized he wouldn't go indefinitely without getting in touch with her. Unfortunately, her marriage had been announced in all the papers, and because Barry would know she was living in Atlanta it would take him a while to gather his courage and contact her at Ethan's house. But she had no doubt that he would call her, and since it was past the time Ethan should be at work, she knew this could very well be him.

"Savannah?" Wallace Jeffries said, his voice booming to her as if he were in the other room rather than at the offices of his law firm hundreds of miles away in Maryland.

"Yes, it's me. Good morning, Mr. Jeffries."

"I just got into my office, but the first thing I saw when I arrived was your paperwork from the clinic where your brother was a nurse. I can fax it to you right now if you like.''

Savannah sat up, licked her lips. The wonderful after-glow of making love with Ethan had vanished and in its place was a horrible feeling of dread. But she knew why. She was about to see evidence that her brother had forged Ethan's signature, and though Ethan wasn't pressing charges Savannah knew seeing the proof of Barry's crime would be difficult.

"Let me put you on hold while I go to the den to get Ethan's fax number."

After racing to her room to grab her robe, Savannah ran to the den. She picked up the phone and read Ethan's fax number to her attorney. Replacing the receiver in its cradle, the sense of doom again overcame her and again she quashed it. It was time to start thinking about Barry and how to bring him home with the least amount of fuss. She hoped there would be something on the papers that would somehow make him look less guilty in Ethan's eyes. Though he wasn't pressing charges, Savannah knew it might not be easy for him to forgive Barry for what he had done. But she wanted her family to be a family. She couldn't spend the rest of her life without her brother, and she was now committed to Ethan. They had to get along.

Still, she knew there was plenty of time to think about that when the fax arrived, so she decided to shower and dress, then have breakfast with her husband. But while she was in the shower, Ethan poked his head in her bathroom and explained that because he was late he was leaving without eating. Feeling devilish, she almost suggested he join her rather than go to work, but she suddenly remembered the odd look in his eyes when she awakened and how quickly he had jumped out of bed, and a new dread assaulted her. Every other morning he had stayed around. Now, suddenly, because she had let him make love to her, he was leaving without breakfast.

No, she thought. She wasn't going to let hormones get to her. Ethan might not have said it, but he loved her.

As soon as she was dressed, she went to the den and yanked the fax from the machine. On her way to the dining room she scanned the pages. The first was the release form on which Barry allegedly forged Ethan's signature. The next few pages had to do with her own releases, authorizations and directions. Those she skimmed after asking Joni for oatmeal and wheat toast.

But when she came to the last page, the page that had the technician's handwritten notes from the procedure and read the control number for the sperm donor, her heart stopped.

Unless someone had made a mistake and written an eight where they meant a three, or unless somebody had incredibly terrible penmanship, it wasn't Ethan's sperm used to create her child.

Without waiting for Joni, she bounced off her chair and ran to the den. She hit the automatic redial to get Wallace Jeffries and within seconds he came on the line.

"Wallace," she said, fear lacing her voice with panic. "Have you reviewed these papers?"

"Briefly."

"The control numbers don't match."

"What? What control numbers? What are you talking about?"

Savannah drew a quick breath to calm herself so she could speak clearly. "The actual procedure paper for my in vitro fertilization lists a different number than the control number on the authorization sheet on which Barry forged Ethan's signature."

"Okay, let me take a look," Wallace said, his voice calm and soothing.

She heard the rustle of papers, then Wallace's short intake of breath not as if he were surprised, but as if he was thinking. "I don't know, Savannah, the computer generated number is very clear. It looks like the kind of label labs create to paste on documents and corresponding samples to assure accuracy, so that one's okay."

"I know. It's the handwritten number that's in question."

"I can see why," Wallace agreed. "That's probably the worst handwriting I've seen in ages."

"So what do you think?"

"I think that if Barry says he shifted Ethan's sperm for use by the clinic the day you were impregnated, then that's what happened."

Savannah looked at the sheets before her. "Barry didn't say he used Ethan's sperm. He left before he could say anything. He ran when he realized my procedure was being audited." She paused, sifting through the papers in front of her, but when she moved on to the last page, the form from the actual procedure, the handwritten eight became clearer and clearer to her. "Wallace, that number is not a three."

"And Ethan's computer generated number is clearly a three. But, Savannah, that form was filled out in the procedure room. In the thick of things a technician might have made a mistake."

Savannah swallowed. "Or they could have used the donor form I originally filled out. Ethan was not my first choice. I had already completed all the paperwork when Barry told me they had a new donor, somebody with a much better profile and at the last minute he got me to fill out a second donor selection form to change my choice. He told me not to worry that it was past the deadline for my paperwork, he would get it to my file. What if he didn't?''

Wallace patiently said, ''Okay, I can understand your concern, but in order to get a warrant for your brother's arrest, the police, a district attorney and a judge had to go over these forms. If they believe that number is a three, I believe that number is a three, and you should believe that number is a three.''

''I can't.''

''Savannah...''

''Mr. Jeffries, my marriage to Ethan McKenzie is predicated on a forgery and a theft. Now, you tell me you want me to continue that marriage based on a possible mistake.''

''You're thinking somebody made a mistake?''

''It's possible that somebody had my original application. I wouldn't let Barry in the room with me when the procedure was performed. What if he thought I would? What if he switched all the copies of the form but the last one? I know you probably think I'm crazy, but I have to check this out.''

Wallace quietly said, ''Okay. I'll make some phone calls.'' He paused, then added, ''Are you going to be okay?''

''Yeah,'' she said, but even she heard the quiver in her voice, as terror trembled through her. This could potentially change everything.

After listening to a few comforting words from Wallace, she disconnected the call and rose from the desk chair and began to pace, hugging herself as if to ward off a chill.

But try as she might she couldn't shake the obvious fear. If this wasn't Ethan's baby, their marriage was over.

Just like with Drew, once Ethan discovered it wasn't his baby in her womb, he wouldn't want her anymore.

She told herself not to think like that, but she couldn't help it. She had committed to Ethan the night before, he had not committed to her. Oh, he had taken some very good steps, and Savannah had laid the foundation of trust, but he hadn't committed to her. And this morning he was different. Very different than what he had been. He wasn't a loving suitor trying to seduce her anymore. He had her. He knew he had her. He didn't have to work to get her to like him. He didn't have to pretend he liked her. And once he discovered that this baby belonged to someone else he wouldn't want her anymore.

The truth of it made her shudder. She could be pregnant with the child of a man she didn't know. Someone Ethan didn't know. A complete stranger. When she was on her own, it hadn't mattered. In some ways, it was what she wanted because it cut down the complications. Now that she was in love, she wanted Ethan's baby.

She sat at the desk and willed herself to cry, to release some of the oppressive emotion, but she couldn't cry. She was too stunned to cry. She was too scared to cry.

Also, as Wallace had said she could be worrying for nothing. In a few hours she would know the truth and then she might be laughing at her overly suspicious concerns...or else she would cry. Maybe scream. Probably run. But for now she couldn't do anything but wait.

Though Wallace thought it would take approximately one hour to contact the clinic and get back to her, he hadn't called by three. So she phoned him, calmly reminding him that she had to tell Ethan something when he got home at four, but inside her heart beat frantically. Wallace told her that the clinic advised they needed hours, maybe days to track down what had happened and though Savannah froze with fear, thinking they were stalling, Wallace continued to be unconcerned.

"At this point, Savannah, my best advice to you as your lawyer is not to say anything to Mr. McKenzie until we have something concrete. Right now, even I think you're panicking for nothing."

"I don't know."

"No, you don't," Wallace insisted. "Right now, you don't *know* anything. All you have is a suspicion and some really poor handwriting. I still say that if the police didn't pick up on that number then there is no mistake. Do Mr. McKenzie a favor and don't put him through what you're going through when this could be nothing but the result of sloppy handwriting."

Wallace's confidence boosted Savannah's confidence somewhat, but she also knew everything about this situation was wrong, out of sync. Her usually trustworthy brother had committed forgery and theft. A man who hadn't looked twice at her during the two years she had worked for him suddenly asked her to marry him. She fit in to a life that was so foreign to her she couldn't even imagine it. Nothing about this situation went the way it was supposed to, so she wasn't surprised that an odd number would send her into a tailspin. And because nothing about this situation followed a normal, predictable pattern, she felt compelled to check it out.

She hung up the phone and fell back on the tall leather office chair, but before she even had a chance to catch her breath, Ethan walked into the den. "Early."

"Yeah, I'm a little early," Ethan said, though Savannah hadn't intended to make that comment aloud. He walked over and kissed her forehead, then pulled her out of the chair and into his arms so he could kiss her appropriately. "Yesterday was a big day for us, a turning point, and it scared me a little. That's why I was quiet this morning. I'm sorry I left before breakfast. I wish I hadn't."

Savannah searched his face and saw real affection for her, and she wished he hadn't left before breakfast, too. She wished he hadn't gone at all. She wished Wallace hadn't called. She wished she hadn't looked at the papers…hell, she wished she hadn't even requested them.

She drew in a quick breath to stop her thoughts. Just as Wallace said, she could be exaggerating that number because she was scared. There was no point in panicking Ethan.

If this baby was his, she didn't just *want* to go forward with this relationship, they *needed* to go forward. Yet she couldn't help but see the other side of the equation. If the baby wasn't his, then she had to face the fact that she would be alone.

Again.

Because she knew Ethan didn't love her. He loved the mother of his child and she wasn't the mother of his child. If they stayed together, she would not only be asking him to face the disappointment of knowing he hadn't created the McKenzie heir he so desperately wanted. She would also be asking him to raise another man's child.

Chapter Eleven

Savannah managed to get through dinner by convincing herself that Wallace was right. If the police and a district attorney hadn't questioned that number, who was she to say there was a mistake? If she were to tell Ethan, particularly since he had already once accused her of getting the paperwork to try to wiggle out of their deal, he might think she was doing it again. Especially when her suspicions seemed so ridiculous.

But when they shifted to the nursery to inspect the progress and began talking about the baby, Savannah's fears resurrected. How could she talk about the baby, how could she pretend everything was fine, when it might not be?

"You do realize, of course, if this is a boy I'm probably going to have to cut my work schedule in half."

Glad for the distraction of that odd conclusion, Savannah laughed. "In half?"

"I hear a lot of complaining from people at work about soccer, T-ball, Little League baseball, basketball..."

"They complain about sports?"

"No, they complain because they don't have enough time. They can't go to every activity. And it makes them mad."

"Oh."

"And," Ethan said, walking across the newly laid white tile floor to loop his arms around Savannah's waist and pull her closer, "since we have money, I've been thinking that there's no point to me working as much as I do. I think maybe the thing for me to do would be to continue to work for Hilton, but as a consultant, rather than in-house counsel."

Savannah laughed again. "I think you think too much. This baby isn't even born yet and already you're taking time off to go to soccer games."

"I want to," Ethan said simply, easily. "I don't want to miss a minute."

She tried to stop the thought that sprang to mind, but she couldn't. It was too obvious. Ethan might love her, but he loved her first and foremost as the mother of his child.

What if this wasn't his child?

Shaking her head in confusion, she stepped out of his arms, ambled to the window and ran her fingers along the smooth new wood used to rebuild the window seat.

"Ethan, it's really great that you love this baby," she said slowly, cautiously, trying not to alert him to the possibility that something might be wrong, because she was the only one who doubted that handwritten number. Even her own attorney thought she was borrowing trouble. Yet things that had seemed so easy and natural the day before, suddenly seemed disordered and muddled. "But I think we both better slow down. We jumped into this thing like there was no tomorrow...."

''There wasn't a tomorrow. We needed to cover up the scandal to protect my father.''

''I know,'' she said. ''It's just that there are a lot of things that could go wrong.''

Ethan seemed to freeze in place. ''Did something happen? Are you sick?'' he asked urgently.

She shook her head. ''No. No,'' she hastily assured him. ''I'm fine.''

''Oh, I get it,'' he said. Again, he walked over and looped his arms around her, pulling her close enough to hold, but not so close that he couldn't see her face. ''This,'' he said, pointing back and forth between them, indicating their relationship, ''happened too fast.''

The minute he said the words, Savannah knew that was true. Not because she didn't love him, but because he didn't love her. Or at least he wasn't as sure of his love as she was of hers. Even he admitted he had left quickly that morning because he was scared, and that was the problem. That might even be why she had built exaggerated concerns around a sloppily written number. She knew that morning when he left that he was behaving oddly, and she also knew their relationship still hinged on this baby. If there was even the slightest possibility this child wasn't his, given Ethan's doubts, Savannah knew she couldn't commit to loving him because he would leave her like Drew had left her.

''Yes. I think things between us are moving too fast.''

''You don't want to sleep with me anymore?''

She shrugged. ''I don't know.''

''Savannah, I know you're confused…''

''I'm more than confused, Ethan. There are lots of things that we didn't consider and I'm afraid that because we jumped into sleeping together we're going to make a mess of everything.''

"I already admitted I left this morning because I was afraid," he said quietly, humbly, so honestly it broke her heart that she had rushed things. "So, maybe we should...well...maybe take things a little more slowly?"

Relief poured through her. "I'd like that."

"I guess in a way, I would, too." He paused, drew in a long, deep breath. "I'm sorry, Savannah, I don't mean to make it sound like I don't trust you. I guess I just don't trust marriage very much."

"I know," she said and ran her fingers along his cheek as guilt and unhappiness swamped her. It almost seemed as if they were doomed. Not because of the baby, but because of their pasts. The way his ex-wife had treated him would affect every decision he made, just as surely as the way Drew had rejected her would affect her decisions, too.

At least they would until she was sure Ethan loved her for herself.

Sad, but resigned, Savannah stretched on her tiptoes and kissed him. "I'll miss you tonight."

He laughed against her mouth. "I don't see why, I'm not going anywhere."

"You know what I mean. We won't be sleeping together."

"Sure we will. We just won't be having sex."

That stopped her. "Oh."

He slid his index finger under her chin and lifted her face until she was looking at him. "You have a problem with that?"

With so many things to consider, Savannah wasn't sure what was right anymore. "I don't know."

"I'm willing to give up the sex for a few weeks because I suspect it's probably the best thing to do for more reasons than just making sure we're not rushing into anything. But I won't give up being close to you.''

Overcome with emotion, Savannah blinked up at him. It was the nicest thing anybody had ever said to her and she knew why he had said it. He loved her. The very fact that he was afraid proved he wasn't going into this as flippantly as he had wanted to when he first suggested that they make this arrangement permanent. He couldn't say it, but when he could he would mean it. And hearing it would make the wait worthwhile.

She rose to her tiptoes again. Kissed him again. ''I think that's a good idea.''

That night, though both wore pajamas to bed, they were very happy. But Ethan couldn't lie ten minutes bound by the two confining pieces of material.

''Savannah, don't take this the wrong way, but I've got to get out of these pajamas.''

She giggled. ''What are you talking about?''

''They're driving me crazy. I always sleep naked.''

That made her out-and-out laugh and he turned and stared at her. ''Why is that funny?''

''I don't know. It just sounds odd.''

He knew that was what he liked about her. That everything was funny, or unusual, or wonderful because she never encountered such wealth, never had servants, never lived with a man. He knew there had been other lovers in her life. He knew she had tried things, experimented, even taken care of herself completely by running her own business. But he always had the sense with her that though other relationships had gone before this one, this one was her best. Her favorite.

He leaned over and kissed her. ''Stop laughing at my misery.''

"Stop being silly, and take off your pajamas."

He sighed as if put upon, if only to hear her laugh again, then hoisted himself off the bed and undid the buttons of his pajama top, tossing the shirt to a convenient chair. Without thought, without preamble, he hooked his thumbs under the waistband of the bottoms and slid them to the floor. He left them lying in a puddle by the bed, and turned to slide under the covers again. But as he reached down to grab the corner of the comforter, he saw Savannah looking at him and he stopped.

"This arrangement isn't going to work if you continue to look at me as if I'm dinner and you're starving."

Her eyes grew huge with embarrassment and she quickly shifted them from his male anatomy to his face. "Sorry."

But Ethan only laughed. He threw himself onto the bed, and—careful with her because of the baby, but also because she was so much smaller than he was—he rolled beside her, wrapped his arms around her and plucked her onto his stomach.

"What are you doing!"

"Making you laugh. I love to hear you laugh."

"Well, I love to laugh, so that's good. But right now I'm exhausted and I need my sleep. Roll me back down."

"I don't think so."

He could have said, "I love you," right then and there. He really could have. There was nothing about her he didn't like and so many things about her he did like that he could have said the words right then and there. But something stopped him. First, he was respectful of Savannah's very real concern that everything was happening too fast between them. Second, he hadn't forgotten his own personal vow to himself, not to get involved again until he was sure. If Savannah was having even the tiniest doubt, he wouldn't say the words that would hurt him later.

He rolled her to her side of the bed again. "Go to sleep," he whispered, and she quickly closed her eyes as if wanting to make sure he didn't do something else.

But he watched her. When her breathing became slow and even, when he was sure she was so deeply asleep that she wouldn't realize what he was doing, he leaned over and studied the delicate features of her face and knew, in his heart, that he loved her.

And he also knew that if he lost her, if something happened, it would be worse than when he lost Lisa.

A month later when Wallace finally called, Savannah had almost forgotten there was a problem.

"Savannah," Wallace said in his smooth, comforting voice. "I'm sorry but the clinic hasn't returned any of my calls for the past month."

"Oh," Savannah said, finding it difficult to muster concern because things were going so well with Ethan and also because she had herself convinced that she'd exaggerated that number. "Why not?"

"Well, I have two thoughts. The first is that the clinic has decided to avoid me indefinitely, maybe even on advice of counsel because though Ethan signed papers saying he wouldn't file a lawsuit you never did…and I'm your attorney. So they may have apprehensions.

"My second thought isn't so kind because if what I'm thinking is true, barring avoiding me, the only other possible reason the clinic hasn't called is that they found something wrong."

Savannah fell to the chair in disbelief. "What?"

"And if they found something wrong, it's also fairly

safe to assume that since Ethan can't sue and I'm the attorney who is poking around, whatever information the clinic uncovered it involves you.''

"Dear God.''

"Savannah, think this through with me,'' Wallace said gently. "What's the only thing for which you could sue these people?''

"I don't know.''

"Negligence. Which in this case would be giving you the wrong sperm. And since your last instructions indicated that you wanted Mr. McKenzie's sperm, the obvious conclusion is that your request wasn't honored…and there's your grounds for a suit.''

Every muscle in Savannah froze. "This might not be Ethan's baby?''

"Savannah, we're only hypothesizing here. We're making an educated guess about why they won't let me see any more papers than what we already have. I could be dead wrong.''

"But you don't think so?'' Savannah whispered as tears pooled in her eyes because her greatest fear was becoming reality. This might not be Ethan's baby.

"I don't know what to think, but I do know the only way we'll find the truth is to file a lawsuit, if only so we can initiate discovery, which they will be forced to answer.''

"You don't think they could be avoiding us for the first reason you said?''

"It's possible. It's also possible that they lost the papers. But not likely.''

"Okay, I'll tell Ethan tonight,'' Savannah said, then choked back a sob. Her worst nightmare was coming true. Except after another month of living together as man and wife for real she had the hope, however slim, that Ethan might love her enough that he wouldn't leave her.

"I'm sorry," Wallace said. "I wish there was another way to do this."

"Me, too."

"The whole hell of it is, you don't know for sure this isn't Mr. McKenzie's baby. But we aren't going to find out until we get the ball rolling with this discovery."

"Or until we do DNA tests."

"Or until your brother comes home," Wallace said casually, then his voice changed. "Or until your brother comes home," he repeated as if inspired. "Savannah! Your brother is the other way to get to the bottom of this. We could hire a private investigator to find your brother and ask him what happened."

Flabbergasted by the wonderful simplicity of the plan, Savannah fell to Ethan's desk chair. "That's a great idea."

"And it kills two birds with one stone. I imagine you're worried about him."

"I am."

"Okay, then, don't talk to Ethan tonight. Give me two weeks with a private investigator. If we haven't found your brother by then, or if he can't confirm this is Ethan's child, then we'll tell Ethan, and get the ball rolling on a lawsuit."

Because Wallace's plan didn't merely solve the problem of the baby, but also brought home her brother, Savannah hung up the phone feeling a little better, but not really good. She was upset about the possibility that the clinic was hiding something, but more than that she knew she should tell Ethan. When her suspicion was only based on a poorly written number, she could excuse keeping the situation a secret from Ethan. But now that the clinic was behaving mysteriously she couldn't shake the feeling that Ethan should know what was going on.

To keep herself occupied, she asked Joni to make another picnic lunch but instead of taking it to Ethan's office, she, Joni and Lewis worked all afternoon, dragging potted trees and every available plant into the den, turning the room into a forest that really looked more like a jungle. They moved furniture and spread a blanket in the middle of a circle of potted trees.

When Ethan came home and saw the mess he almost fainted, but when he realized the trouble Savannah had gone to, he hugged her.

"So, we're having a picnic?"

She nervously fidgeted with the collar of her maternity blouse, then walked over to take a seat on the blanket. "A real one."

"I can see that."

He dropped his briefcase on the desk, then removed his suit coat and draped it across the back of the chair. As he did, he saw the name of a detective agency scrawled on a memo pad.

"What's this?"

Savannah's face puckered in confusion and that puzzled him, then froze him with fear. He had used a detective to find Lisa when she ran to Oregon. He had also used a detective to scout out Lisa's financial holdings because he needed ammunition to keep her from taking half his personal fortune. As far as he was concerned private detectives and divorces went hand in hand. He picked up the notepad and waved it. "What's this?"

She swallowed. "My attorney Wallace Jeffries suggested that I might need the services of that gentleman."

"Why?"

She faltered and Ethan's heart squeezed with pain until she whispered, "I'm trying to find my brother."

Then his anger disappeared, his fear evaporated. Still, he had to wait for his heart rate to calm down before he could apologize. "Savannah, I'm sorry."

She nodded.

"It's just that…well…my ex-wife really did a number on me." He fell to the leather sofa. "God, I'm sorry. I'm so sorry. I shouldn't always punish you for things she did."

Savannah didn't say anything. Instead, she licked her lips and turned away. When she did all of Ethan's negative intuitions sprang to life again.

"You're not divorcing me, but something is wrong."

She drew a long breath.

Ethan's chest filled with air to the point that it hurt. "What?" he asked quietly, calmly, but inside he was melting with pain and fear.

"Ethan," she said, her voice shaking, her hands shaking. "I got the papers from the clinic."

"And."

"And, well, the clinic…the clinic," she stopped because she started to cry and Ethan couldn't help it, he sprang from the sofa and went over and sat beside her on the floor so he could pull her into his arms.

"Shh. Don't worry. Whatever it is we'll deal with it. But, Savannah, if your brother forged my signature it wouldn't surprise me that he did others. And if he did others, he's going to have to pay the consequences."

She looked at him. Tears had made trails on her cheeks. Her eyes were red and water rimmed her lashes. "You think he did something else wrong?"

"How can I not? I know he's your brother and I know

you love him, but you're going to have to deal with him honestly."

"What are you saying?"

"I'm saying that it didn't feel right for me to let him off the hook for forging my signature and creating my child without my consent. If he did something else wrong, something for which he will be punished, at least we can both have the security of knowing we didn't teach him that he can break the law with impunity."

"He didn't do anything else," Savannah said and pushed out of his arms. Because she was obviously upset with him, Ethan expected her to run out of the room. Instead she paced to the window.

"Then what is wrong? Why are you crying? Why are you scaring me to death?"

She turned, and through a voice deepened by tears she whispered, "I got the papers from the clinic. Everything pertaining to my in vitro fertilization has a computer generated sticker on it that has *your* control number on it, except the final paper. That number is handwritten, as if there was no sheet of control numbers to use."

"And that number's different?" he asked confused.

"We don't know. Because it's handwritten, and because the handwriting is very sloppy, there's one questionable digit."

"But it's handwritten," Ethan said slowly, dully, his heart in such pain he wasn't sure he could breathe because he knew what this meant. One wrong number and their baby wouldn't be his. "It could very easily be human error."

She swallowed hard. "Yes. But that's not the end of it. My attorney has been trying to get information from the clinic, but they won't return his calls. He thinks that after his initial contact, which alerted them to the number difference and forced them to investigate, they found something…something pertaining to me…something about which I could sue…and that's why they aren't calling him. They aren't going to hand him the ammo to make the case. Wallace thinks they are forcing him to file a suit."

"And you think that what they discovered is the difference in the numbers."

"My lawyer thinks that the only reason I could sue the clinic would be because they didn't fulfill my wishes and use the donor I requested." She swallowed. "Because you were my choice, that means they used someone else's sperm." She paused again to swallow tears. "Ethan, I'm sorry."

"Yeah, me too," he said, his voice deceptively calm as his entire world crashed in around him. He might not have a baby. He wouldn't be a dad. "How long have you known?"

She swallowed, and he could see from the look on her face that she knew that that was the real problem. She opened her mouth to speak, but he stopped her with a wave of his hand.

"You don't have to tell me. You found out the morning after we made love." He shook his head. "Jeez, what a chump."

"Ethan," she said desperately. "You're not a chump."

"Oh, really? Then why didn't you tell me?"

She smiled as if relieved. "My lawyer didn't think I should. He didn't want you to worry the way we were worrying…."

"Oh, Savannah, don't think that saves you! It makes things worse," he yelled, then stalked away. "Your attorney wasn't trying to protect me. He was protecting you.... Or should I say your child support. He knew that the minute I discovered this isn't my baby, all bets would be off. You wouldn't get a dime."

She gasped as if he slapped her. "That's not how it is!"

"Really? That's how it looks to me. You thought you found a mistake, but instead of telling me, and possibly screwing up your deal here, you investigated on your own. And your attorney advised you not to tell me. Now why would he do that? And why would you even ask him if you should tell me?" he asked rhetorically. "Let's see. Could you be trying to stay here long enough to solidify your position for a divorce settlement even if you lose child support?"

He combed his fingers through his hair and turned away from her. "When will I learn not to trust anybody about anything?" he muttered as insult, pain and humiliation ricocheted through him. He drew a quick breath. "I'm going out. Enjoy your picnic. You've certainly set yourself up well."

Savannah waited until two o'clock for him to come home, but he never did. He didn't come home until after work the next day, and he looked like he'd slept in his suit.

"Hi."

He rubbed his eyes tiredly, then said, "Hi."

"Ethan, I am really sorry."

He held up his hand to stop her. "Don't. I'm not interested in what you have to say or what excuse you think gives you the right to drag me and my family through this because I don't have a clue what the hell you and your brother were trying to prove. But now that we've started this thing we have to keep it going. And that means we have to live together for at least another six weeks. Then we'll get DNA tests. If the baby's mine, we'll work out a visitation agreement before you leave. If the baby's not mine, you don't even come home...understood?''

Savannah swallowed hard, then nodded. ''Yes.'' She understood perfectly, just like with Drew, now that Ethan knew the baby wasn't his he didn't want her.

''Did you ask the cook to make something for dinner?''

She nodded. ''I can't very well starve.''

''No, you can't,'' he agreed, then began walking back to the den. ''I'll be out in time to eat.''

Dinner was solemn and so was breakfast the next morning. For the next week Ethan ate meals with her, but hardly said anything and didn't spend a minute with her that he didn't have to. With every day that passed, Savannah thought she should grow accustomed to his rejection and get stronger, but she didn't. All she wanted to do was sleep. Soon she couldn't even eat.

''You have to eat,'' Ethan said, bringing her dinner up to her room on a tray. Even though he had always known she had no part in the original scheme, she had still kept important information from him and he knew why she had done it. For money. She didn't believe they were falling in love. He had virtually handed her his heart, but the very next day she found the mistake and knew she had to make a choice. Because he vacillated, she didn't believe their relationship stood a chance, so she stopped it, or tried—he would only agree to call a temporary halt to the sexual end of things—in order that she could fulfill the intent of their prenuptial agreement. That document contained no mention of the baby. It was a straightforward marriage contract. All she had to do was stay married to him for six months to earn the nominal settlement they had added so no one would get suspicious. True, it wasn't an enormous sum, but the problem wasn't money. It was the fact that she even considered it. In a sense, when forced into a choice she took the money over him.

He laid the tray on her bed. "It isn't good for you or the baby to go without food. Besides, we have an appointment with Floyd tonight."

"Our last."

"Yep. Our last."

A silence fell over the room and seeing her lying in bed sad, exhausted, so miserable she couldn't even eat, Ethan wished that nothing had changed between them. He wouldn't wish this pain on anyone, but more than that, and in spite of the fact that he didn't believe she loved him, he missed her. He especially missed hearing her laugh.

She scooted up on the bed and he placed the tray across her legs, ready to run because he knew he was vulnerable. He missed her. He was pretty darned sure he loved her. But she didn't love him and he also couldn't trust her. When push came to shove, she preferred money over him.

She picked up the fork and took a bite, then another, and Ethan stepped back a pace for every bite she took. When he got to the door, he didn't wait for her to finish, he simply turned and walked out of the room.

"Hey, Ethan."

Ethan glanced up to see Josh standing in the doorway of his office. "Hey, Josh."

"What are you doing here? It's past seven."

"I have a little extra work..."

Peering at Ethan's nearly clean desk, Josh frowned. "Ethan, you're talking to the master, here. I lived what you're doing for four years. You're not going home because you don't want to. The only thing I can't figure out is why."

Recognizing there was no way out of this conversation, but also realizing he needed somebody to talk to Ethan said, "Close the door."

At that Josh laughed. "Ethan, it's seven o'clock at night. There's nobody here."

"I don't want to take any chances."

"You know, Ethan," Josh said, as he walked to the door, then closed it. "Did you ever stop to think that that's your problem?"

"What? That I hate to have people hear details of my private life?"

"No, that you don't want to take any chances."

"I took chances. Several chances. One with Lisa. One with Savannah. All I get is screwed."

"How do you know?"

Tapping a pencil on his desk, Ethan considered lying, but drew a long breath and said, "Because this baby might not be mine."

Josh's eyes widened and he fell to the chair in front of Ethan's desk. "What?"

"Savannah's in the process of tracking down her brother because the actual sheet from her procedure is so poorly written that we're not sure they used my sperm. There's a number that could be a three or an eight. If it's a three, the baby's mine. If it's an eight, I'm screwed."

"And only her brother knows for sure?"

"Her brother and the clinic. But the clinic's not talking to us. Everybody's hired a lawyer. I think they think that if the baby's mine, I'm going to sue even though I said

I wouldn't. And if it's not mine, I think they're afraid we're going to sue them for starting this whole mess.''

"It is a mess," Josh agreed. "But I'm a little unclear about what this has to do with your feelings about Savannah.''

"She didn't tell me. She figured this out weeks ago, but she kept it from me, because if she stays married to me for six months she gets a settlement.''

Josh frowned. "Really?''

"Not a big one. In the grand scheme of things it's fairly small. She even balked that we were putting it in at all, but it is enough that anybody who saw the thing wouldn't get suspicious.''

"Let me get this straight. She didn't want your money, but you think she changed her mind?''

"That's not as far-fetched as you think. It's what Lisa did. She stayed married to me long enough that she could take me to court to contest our prenuptial agreement. Besides, what other reason would Savannah have for not telling me?''

Josh shook his head. "There could be a million other reasons, but the biggest is that it almost sounds like there was nothing to tell. All anybody has at this point is suspicions.''

"Don't confuse the issue.''

"I don't think I'm the one who's confusing the issue,'' Josh said, shifting on his seat. "I think you are, because there are really two issues here. The first one is the baby. It may or may not be yours.''

"That's a big issue.''

"Yes, it is, but it really doesn't have anything to do with the second issue.''

"I don't see a second issue.''

"The second issue is whether or not you love Savannah."

"She lied to me."

"Not from where I'm sitting. From where I'm sitting you and her brother have batted her around as if she were some kind of soccer ball. We've all agreed that her brother thought he was doing the right thing by assuring Savannah's baby got a good father. But can you say your motives were as pure? You treated her like solid gold while you thought she was carrying your child. But at the first sign of trouble, the very first sign because no one's really proven this child isn't yours, you pinned Lisa's character traits and motives on Savannah because it was easier than trusting her, and you dropped her like a hot potato." With that he rose. "You know what, Ethan? If I were Savannah I would be so angry with you and her brother that *I* would refuse to see either one of you again. You think about that for a while."

He did. In the quiet of his office, with the echoing stillness of loneliness surrounding him, Ethan thought about it long and hard and soon he saw what Josh was saying. Because he was prepared to be hurt, prepared to be cheated, he hadn't thought the situation through. He attributed all of Lisa's bad character traits to Savannah, and judged her through that filter so he could shove her out of his life. All without proof.

The truth smothered him in guilt, almost suffocating him. He couldn't believe he had been so foolish. But he had been. And he had to fix it.

He rushed home and found Savannah in the den, staring out the wall of windows behind his desk.

"Savannah?"

She turned from the window and he could see her eyes were red and swollen from crying.

"We found my brother. He arrived in Atlanta this morning."

His heart stopped, his breathing stopped. Because she had been crying, he was positive he knew the verdict, and he was equally positive he wasn't ready to hear it. "Where is he?"

"Away from you," Savannah said, then seemed to choke on a sob. "Which is exactly where I intend to be, too, once we have this discussion."

"The baby's not mine."

"The baby *is* yours. But I don't want to live here anymore. I don't want to see you anymore. I don't want to have anything to do with you anymore."

"Savannah, don't. I'm sorry." He rushed to her side, turned her away from the window and enfolded her in his arms. "Dear God, I am sorry. I talked with Josh tonight and he made me realize what I had put you through. The only excuse I have is that..."

"Ethan, the only excuse you have is that you don't love me. Just like I told you in the beginning, you loved the idea of having a baby. You loved me as the mother. But you didn't love me. And I can't do this anymore."

"Savannah, please, listen to me," Ethan said, shifting her away enough that he could look into her eyes. "I do love you."

"No, you don't."

"Yes, I do."

"No, you don't," she shouted and wrestled her way out of his arms. "Don't you see! In the first place, you put me in an awful position. Marry you or see my brother go to jail. Then you treated me so well I couldn't help but fall in love with you. Then we slept together. And then when things weren't exactly what you thought they should be, you blamed me."

"It wasn't that I thought you did anything, it was that I thought you didn't trust me enough to tell me."

"That's a convenient excuse for the fact that when push came to shove, you didn't really want me unless I was giving you a baby. Well, now I'm giving you a baby. Except now I don't want you." As she said the last she rounded the desk and because of her burdened tummy began an awkward half run to the door.

"Savannah! Wait!"

But Savannah didn't stop. She plowed past him, shrugging out of his hold when he tried to catch her. She stormed to the door and began to barrel through but suddenly, as if she had hit a wall, she came to a crashing halt. She grabbed the door frame and moaned.

Ethan rushed over. "Oh, my God, Savannah, are you okay?"

"I'm fine," she said, but she began panting the way Floyd had taught her.

"You're in labor?"

She drew a quick cleansing breath. "Ethan, I'm not just in labor. My water broke. Call an ambulance."

"Lewis will—"

"I don't want Lewis! I don't want you! Call an ambulance."

Chapter Twelve

Using training given by Floyd, Ethan decided to ignore Savannah's wishes and quickly called Lewis who drove them to the hospital. While she was in with nurses getting her preliminary care, he found a private space and phoned his parents. By the time the call was complete, Savannah was ready for his company and he walked into the labor room.

"Hey," he said, leaning over the bed to kiss her forehead.

"Hey," she said, smiling slightly, but Ethan also noticed that she shifted away from him.

Knowing he deserved that, he held back a wince and asked, "So, what's going on?"

"The pains are very close," she said, grimacing, which alerted Ethan to the fact that she was having another. "But since my water only leaked out, didn't gush out, the general consensus is that there is nothing to worry about. My doctor's been called."

"Sounds like everything's under control, then," Ethan

said, remembering to stay calm and casual as Floyd had taught.

"Yes, everything's fine," Savannah said, trying to mimic his composure, but Ethan could see she was talking through gritted teeth.

"Are you having a contraction?"

She panted out a few breaths, then said, "Yes."

"Then, Savannah, you've got to breathe."

"I am breathing...."

"No, you have to do the hee-hee-hee, who-who-who stuff, remember?" he said, sliding his arm under her shoulder. "What kind of contraction is it?"

"It is a really, really enormous pain!" Savannah said, jerking herself away from him. "And right now, it's over."

She didn't say, "So get away from me," but Ethan could hear it in her tone. Realizing she didn't want him near her hurt like a slap across the cheek, but given everything that had happened in the past few weeks, he understood. He had nearly ruined their relationship, but he planned to fix it. He wasn't leaving her, and he wasn't letting her leave him. They were going to raise this baby together and he was also determined to help bring it into the world.

But as the hours wore on with Savannah continually asking him to leave, refusing his coaching for her breathing and being downright angry that he was in the room, Ethan's patience began to wear thin.

Finally, at about two o'clock in the morning, a nurse walked in and said, "Mr. McKenzie?"

Ethan jumped from his chair. "Yes."

"Your parents are here."

"My *parents* are here?"

Smiling broadly, the nurse nodded. "Parker McKenzie

can't hide who he is. They said they've been driving all night from D.C.''

"Oh, great," Ethan said, but he walked to the bed on which Savannah lay. "Let me go check this out."

"Why don't you take them to your house?" Savannah asked and Ethan knew that she was really asking him to leave. But sweat had beaded on her brow from the work and pain of labor and she was exhausted. Whether she wanted to admit it or not, she needed him.

He smoothed the hair from her temple. "Savannah, I'm here for you."

"I know but you don't have to be. Everything I'm going through is perfectly normal."

"True, but that doesn't make it any less difficult."

She grimaced with pain, but still managed to smile and instead of feeling guilty as he had the other times, Ethan felt frustrated. But not with her, with himself. He had this whole relationship sown up but he blew it. Now she wouldn't look at him, wouldn't talk to him, wouldn't accept his help.

He ran his fingers through her hair again. "This is our baby, you know."

She shrugged. "Our baby, but my mistake. Ethan, I would never cut you out of this child's life. Never. I love that you are this baby's father. I don't think he or she could ask for a better parent. But just like you said, I didn't trust you. I wasn't honest with you. Which proves we don't belong together. So why don't you go? I would prefer to handle my part alone. Then from here on out our lawyers can sort through everything...."

She gasped and lifted her shoulders off the bed and Ethan suspected a particularly strong contraction must have overcome her. He reached out to try to help her. "Savannah..."

"No, please," she said, shrugging out of his hold and motioning for the nurse. "I don't want you here."

"Savannah!"

"Go!" she yelled, then she moaned in pain. The nurse rushed to her side, shifting her to lessen the pain and Ethan stood by helplessly.

The nurse glanced at him. "Why don't you take a break? Go see your parents. I'll call you if anything happens."

Frustrated, confused, Ethan wandered out into the hall. He pushed through a pair of swinging doors that took him out of the private labor and delivery section and into the family waiting area. His parents spotted him immediately and rushed to greet him.

"What's happening?"

Ethan ran his hand across the back of his neck. "She's okay. A little grouchy, hyper—"

His mother gave him a sly look. "She doesn't want you in the room, does she?"

He shook his head.

"Don't feel bad," Penny said, leading Ethan to one of the plastic chairs along the wall of the waiting room. "I did the same thing to your father after a few hours of pain. I'm going to take a look around to see if I can find a vending machine to get you some coffee because it's going to be a long night. Your father can relate his side of the story to you while I'm gone."

Neither Ethan nor his father said anything as his mother walked down the hall, pressed the button for the elevator and waited for its arrival. Once the doors swooshed closed behind her, Parker McKenzie turned to his son.

"You did something, didn't you?"

Ethan laughed.

"I know you did, because that's why your mother kicked me out when she was in labor with you. I said something stupid." He shook his head. "After hours and hours of labor, I was every bit as tired as she was. She got a pain that must have been unexpectedly awful and she screamed." He paused again, but this time it was to catch Ethan's gaze. "Now, remember, I was tired, too."

Knowing he was about to hear something good, Ethan nodded. "So what did you say?"

Parker sighed. "I said, 'Oh, come on, it can't hurt that bad.'"

Ethan burst out laughing. "You didn't!"

"I did."

"I'm surprised she didn't shoot you."

"She will remember it until the day we die."

Thinking of Savannah's current state of mind, Ethan said, "I have no doubt about that."

"So what stupid thing did you say to Savannah?"

"I didn't say anything…."

"Oh, come on. Women aren't as irrational as men in bars and on golf courses paint them to be. I know you said or did something."

Ethan swallowed. He was tired. He was confused. And he had been for the past four months…well, actually only for two months. The first two months of his marriage had been the happiest months of his life.

"I didn't say anything today," Ethan said slowly, cautiously. "But a few weeks ago, we had a…'situation' and I accused her of lying to me."

"Lying about what?"

"Dad, this is a really long story and I'm not sure this is the time to get into it."

"Well, would it help if I told you that somebody in

the National Committee discovered a little trouble her brother got into at the clinic where he used to work?''

Ethan glanced up sharply. ''You know?''

''Everything except whether or not this is a real marriage. If it's a fake the two of you are very convincing when you kiss.''

''We were trying to protect you.''

''So was the committee member.'' Parker patted Ethan's hand. ''Don't worry. It's a dead story. But I'm guessing that whatever you accused Savannah of lying about it had to do with her brother and the sperm bank.''

''She discovered what she thought was an error in the paperwork that might have proved I wasn't the baby's father. But she didn't tell me right away and I got angry that she lied. By the time I figured out she hadn't lied, she really was trying to protect me and that I loved her...it was too late.''

''Do you?''

''Do I what?''

''Love her?''

Ethan sighed and combed his fingers through his hair. ''Yes. Damn it. Yes.''

''And did you tell her this?''

''I told her once.''

''What happened?''

''She didn't believe me.''

''You have really screwed this up royally.''

''No kidding.''

''So what are you going to do?''

''I don't have a clue. This is the worst possible time to try to straighten this out. She needs me but won't accept my help. I think that about sums up how much she hates me.''

''Or it could be your perfect opportunity.''

"Yeah, right."

"I'm serious. She needs you, but she keeps issuing you away, and you keep listening like you're not smart enough to help her in spite of her warnings."

Ethan looked at his father through narrowed eyes. "What the hell are you talking about?"

"She's telling you to leave because she feels you don't want to be there. You've got to prove that you do want to be there by staying with her through it all, no matter how badly she treats you, because that, son, is how you prove you love somebody. Staying when the going isn't exactly the peaches and cream you married her for."

Ethan rose. "You better be right."

"Of course, I'm right."

Ethan chuckled and began to walk away, but his father stopped him.

"One more thing."

Ethan turned.

"If you really love her and really want to keep this marriage, you're going to have to accept the brother, exactly as he is."

"But he..."

"No, buts." Parker sighed. "Do you think the Democratic National Committee likes Uncle Leo?"

Thinking of Penny McKenzie's younger brother, a professional student until the age of thirty-two, a man who staged demonstrations long after they were popular...a man who once did a beer commercial, Ethan laughed. "No. My guess is they hate him."

"And I've never said a word to the man...do you know why?"

Ethan shook his head.

"Everybody's entitled to make his own mistakes, learn his own lessons. The brother's part of the deal. But to get a good wife and some kids who are probably going to be drop-dead gorgeous, Ethan, I think you can suck it up for a few visits a year.''

Ethan couldn't help it, he laughed. He walked into the labor room laughing, just in time to see Savannah gearing up to handle another pain. He rushed to her side.

She said, ''I'm fine.''

Ethan laughed, then kissed her forehead. ''No, you're not. I mean, you're not sick like you're going to die, but you're in pain and I'm here to help.''

''I don't need...''

''No, you're right. You don't need me. But if you were smart you would want me to be here, because I want to be here.''

''No, you don't.''

''Yes, I do.''

''Okay, you want to see your child born. All right. I understand.''

The pain she had talked her way through seemed to subside and Ethan turned her to face him. ''I want to be here because I love you. *You.* I love the baby. I'll love it even more when it's finally out. But right now, right at this very minute and for the past four months I have loved you. *You.*''

He lifted her slightly by her shoulders so she was high enough that he could kiss her. Because he took her so much by surprise, her mouth relaxed under his and he kissed her as hungrily and greedily as he had the night they consummated their marriage. When he finally pulled away, she stared at him as if dazed.

''And I love you enough that your brother and I are going to start all over again.''

The dazed look evaporated from her eyes and she frowned. ''Right.''

"Hey, I finally figured out I don't even know the guy. I'm judging him by one thing he did—a thing you claim was motivated by his love for you. I was wrong. I apologize."

Savannah only stared at him.

Ethan chuckled. "He can't be as off the wall as my Uncle Leo and my father has put up with him for decades."

Savannah began to laugh but another pain overtook her. This one, Ethan could tell, was far worse than the rest.

"Okay," the nurse said, materializing from the back of the room. "After we ride this one out," she said, sing-songing as she joined Ethan at the side of the bed. "We'll check how far along you are but I have a feeling you're about to become a mother."

"See that," Ethan said, squeezing her fingers, and she surprised him by squeezing back. "In another hour or so we are going to be parents."

"Real parents," she agreed, in between the panting Floyd had taught her.

"A real family," Ethan said, then joined in the rhythm of the panting to keep her focused.

From there everything happened in a blur. The nurse agreed they should page the doctor who had arrived at the hospital and was sleeping in a lounge. He confirmed her assessment that it was time to deliver the baby. Amid the scurrying nurses, calmly conveyed instructions from the doctor and a well-appreciated anesthesiologist, Brandon Ethan McKenzie was born.

Ethan looked at him in amazement. "We have a son."

Savannah smiled sleepily. "Yes, we do."

"So now what?"

"I don't have a clue."

Sally, the nurse who had been with them for the duration laughed. "Now, we take the baby for an exam by your pediatrician, while you go share the good news."

Heeding the nurse's instructions, Ethan walked out into the waiting area in a bit of a daze. "It's a boy."

"A boy!" Penny yelped, then hugged her son. "Finally, another McKenzie male!"

"Congratulations," Parker said. When Penny released Ethan, Parker enfolded him in a big hug but took the opportunity to whisper, "Did you straighten things out?"

Ethan took a long breath. "I think so."

Penny frowned. "Straighten what out?"

"Do you have ears like a cat?" Ethan said, facing his mother.

"No. I'm just perceptive."

Parker shook his head, but he laughed. "I think Ethan's going to have an Uncle Leo in his family."

"Oh," Penny said, grimacing.

"It's not so bad," Ethan said. "I'm not running for anything political."

"See, now that's the spirit," Parker said, slapping his son on the back. "Right now you should go back to the room and be waiting for Savannah when she wakes up. There are no 'I think so's' in marriage. You have to be sure you and Savannah are on the same page...and if you're not," he said, looking Ethan right in the eye, "you better compromise or you're going to lose a very good woman."

Ethan didn't have any doubt about that. In fact, he was so committed, he waited through her nap and then two hours of excited grogginess that followed as he and Savannah alternated between holding the baby and trying to get some sleep. He drifted off on the uncomfortable plastic chair at about six that morning and awakened again at nine to find his wife sitting up in bed, holding the baby, staring at him as if he were the Hope Diamond.

"I can't believe it."

Happy to get out of the uncomfortable chair, Ethan rose. "He is perfect," he said, but he put his finger under Savannah's chin and tilted her face until she was looking at him. "But he's not the main focus of things for a minute. Actually, he's not the main focus of our marriage. I'm sure he'll take up all our time for the next few years...decades," he amended, then he laughed. "But right now I need to clear up a few things." He paused, sighed. "Josh and I had a talk about what happened and he made me see I sort of superimposed Lisa's character traits on you when you told me about the problem. I'm sorry. I know why I did it, but I also know it was wrong, and I also swear I will never do it again."

Savannah nodded.

"With that settled, I'm asking you to marry me for real. For good. Because I love you. If it would make you see our situation differently, I would even be willing to go through an entirely new ceremony."

Savannah pressed her lips together and tears pooled in her eyes. "I don't think so."

"You don't want another ceremony or you don't want to be married to me?"

"I don't need another ceremony." She paused, drew a long breath. "I love you, too, Ethan. I was very happy being married to you until I found out about the mistake and kept the secret. I promise. ."

He pressed his finger to her lips. "You don't have to promise me anything except to love, honor and cherish as long as we both shall live."

She smiled. "I do."

"Then I think we are officially married for real."

So did Savannah. After years and years of being alone, she had finally found love and had her family.

The nurse poked her head inside the room. "Mrs. McKenzie, your brother is here."

Savannah licked her suddenly dry lips, but Ethan laughed. "Send him in."

And then Savannah knew everything was going to be okay. Really okay. For the rest of their lives okay.

She caught Ethan's hand. "I love you."

"I love you, too."

*   *   *   *   *

King Philippe has died, leaving no male heirs to ascend the throne. Until his mother announces that a son *may* exist, embarking everyone on a desperate search for... the missing heir.

Royally Wed
The Missing Heir

Their quest begins March 2002 and continues through June 2002.

On sale March 2002, the emotional
OF ROYAL BLOOD
by Carolyn Zane (SR #1576)

On sale April 2002, the intense
IN PURSUIT OF A PRINCESS
by Donna Clayton (SR #1582)

On sale May 2002, the heartwarming
A PRINCESS IN WAITING
by Carol Grace (SR #1588)

On sale June 2002, the exhilarating
A PRINCE AT LAST!
by Cathie Linz (SR #1594)

Available at your favorite retail outlet.

Silhouette®
Where love comes alive™

Visit Silhouette at www.eHarlequin.com
SRRW4

If you enjoyed what you just read,
then we've got an offer you can't resist!

Take 2 bestselling love stories FREE!
Plus get a FREE surprise gift!

Clip this page and mail it to Silhouette Reader Service™

IN U.S.A.	**IN CANADA**
3010 Walden Ave.	P.O. Box 609
P.O. Box 1867	Fort Erie, Ontario
Buffalo, N.Y. 14240-1867	L2A 5X3

YES! Please send me 2 free Silhouette Romance® novels and my free surprise gift. After receiving them, if I don't wish to receive anymore, I can return the shipping statement marked cancel. If I don't cancel, I will receive 6 brand-new novels every month, before they're available in stores! In the U.S.A., bill me at the bargain price of $3.15 plus 25¢ shipping and handling per book and applicable sales tax, if any*. In Canada, bill me at the bargain price of $3.50 plus 25¢ shipping and handling per book and applicable taxes**. That's the complete price and a savings of at least 10% off the cover prices—what a great deal! I understand that accepting the 2 free books and gift places me under no obligation ever to buy any books. I can always return a shipment and cancel at any time. Even if I never buy another book from Silhouette, the 2 free books and gift are mine to keep forever.

215 SEN DFNQ
315 SEN DFNR

Name _____ (PLEASE PRINT)

Address _____ Apt.#

City _____ State/Prov. _____ Zip/Postal Code

* Terms and prices subject to change without notice. Sales tax applicable in N.Y.
** Canadian residents will be charged applicable provincial taxes and GST.
 All orders subject to approval. Offer limited to one per household and not valid to current Silhouette Romance® subscribers.
 ® are registered trademarks of Harlequin Enterprises Limited.

SROM01   ©1998 Harlequin Enterprises Limited

This Mother's Day Give Your Mom A Royal Treat

Win a fabulous one-week vacation in Puerto Rico for you and your mother at the luxurious Inter-Continental San Juan Resort & Casino. The prize includes round trip airfare for two, breakfast daily and a mother and daughter day of beauty at the beachfront hotel's spa.

INTER·CONTINENTAL
San Juan
RESORT & CASINO

Here's all you have to do:

Tell us in 100 words or less how your mother helped with the romance in your life. It may be a story about your engagement, wedding or those boyfriends when you were a teenager or any other romantic advice from your mother. The entry will be judged based on its originality, emotionally compelling nature and sincerity. See official rules on following page.

Send your entry to:
Mother's Day Contest

In Canada	**In U.S.A.**
P.O. Box 637	P.O. Box 9076
Fort Erie, Ontario	3010 Walden Ave.
L2A 5X3	Buffalo, NY
	14269-9076

Or enter online at www.eHarlequin.com

PRROY

HARLEQUIN MOTHER'S DAY CONTEST 2216
OFFICIAL RULES
NO PURCHASE NECESSARY TO ENTER

Two ways to enter:

• **Via The Internet:** Log on to the Harlequin romance website (www.eHarlequin.com) anytime beginning 12:01 a.m. E.S.T., January 1, 2002 through 11:59 p.m. E.S.T., April 1, 2002 and follow the directions displayed on-line to enter your name, address (including zip code), e-mail address and in 100 words or fewer, describe how your mother helped with the romance in your life.

• **Via Mail:** Handprint (or type) on an 8 1/2" x 11" plain piece of paper, your name, address (including zip code) and e-mail address (if you have one), and in 100 words or fewer, describe how your mother helped with the romance in your life. Mail your entry via first-class mail to: Harlequin Mother's Day Contest 2216, (in the U.S.) P.O. Box 9076, Buffalo, NY 14269-9076; (in Canada) P.O. Box 637, Fort Erie, Ontario, Canada L2A 5X3.

For eligibility, entries must be submitted either through a completed Internet transmission or postmarked no later than 11:59 p.m. E.S.T., April 1, 2002 (mail-in entries must be received by April 9, 2002). Limit one entry per person, household address and e-mail address. On-line and/or mailed entries received from persons residing in geographic areas in which entry is not permissible will be disqualified.

Entries will be judged by a panel of judges, consisting of members of the Harlequin editorial, marketing and public relations staff using the following criteria:
  • Originality - 50%
  • Emotional Appeal - 25%
  • Sincerity - 25%

In the event of a tie, duplicate prizes will be awarded. Decisions of the judges are final.

Prize: A 6-night/7-day stay for two at the Inter-Continental San Juan Resort & Casino, including round-trip coach air transportation from gateway airport nearest winner's home (approximate retail value: $4,000). Prize includes breakfast daily and a mother and daughter day of beauty at the beachfront hotel's spa. Prize consists of only those items listed as part of the prize. Prize is valued in U.S. currency.

All entries become the property of Torstar Corp. and will not be returned. No responsibility is assumed for lost, late, illegible, incomplete, inaccurate, non-delivered or misdirected mail or misdirected e-mail, for technical, hardware or software failures of any kind, lost or unavailable network connections, or failed, incomplete, garbled or delayed computer transmission or any human error which may occur in the receipt or processing of the entries in this Contest.

Contest open only to residents of the U.S. (except Colorado) and Canada, who are 18 years of age or older and is void wherever prohibited by law; all applicable laws and regulations apply. Any litigation within the Province of Quebec respecting the conduct or organization of a publicity contest may be submitted to the Régie des alcools, des courses et des jeux for a ruling. Any litigation respecting the awarding of a prize may be submitted to the Régie des alcools, des courses et des jeux only for the purpose of helping the parties reach a settlement. Employees and immediate family members of Torstar Corp. and D.L. Blair, Inc., their affiliates, subsidiaries and all other agencies, entities and persons connected with the use, marketing or conduct of this Contest are not eligible to enter. Taxes on prize are the sole responsibility of winner. Acceptance of any prize offered constitutes permission to use winner's name, photograph or other likeness for the purposes of advertising, trade and promotion on behalf of Torstar Corp., its affiliates and subsidiaries without further compensation to the winner, unless prohibited by law.

Winner will be determined no later than April 15, 2002 and be notified by mail. Winner will be required to sign and return an Affidavit of Eligibility form within 15 days after winner notification. Non-compliance within that time period may result in disqualification and an alternate winner may be selected. Winner of trip must execute a Release of Liability prior to ticketing and must possess required travel documents (e.g. Passport, photo ID) where applicable. Travel must be completed within 12 months of selection and is subject to traveling companion completing and returning a Release of Liability prior to travel; and hotel and flight accommodations availability. Certain restrictions and blackout dates may apply. No substitution of prize permitted by winner. Torstar Corp. and D.L. Blair, Inc., their parents, affiliates, and subsidiaries are not responsible for errors in printing or electronic presentation of Contest, or entries. In the event of printing or other errors which may result in unintended prize values or duplication of prizes, all affected entries shall be null and void. If for any reason the Internet portion of the Contest is not capable of running as planned, including infection by computer virus, bugs, tampering, unauthorized intervention, fraud, technical failures, or any other causes beyond the control of Torstar Corp. which corrupt or affect the administration, secrecy, fairness, integrity or proper conduct of the Contest, Torstar Corp. reserves the right, at its sole discretion, to disqualify any individual who tampers with the entry process and to cancel, terminate, modify or suspend the Contest or the Internet portion thereof. In the event the Internet portion must be terminated a notice will be posted on the website and all entries received prior to termination will be judged in accordance with these rules. In the event of a dispute regarding an on-line entry, the entry will be deemed submitted by the authorized holder of the e-mail account submitted at the time of entry. Authorized account holder is defined as the natural person who is assigned to an e-mail address by an Internet access provider, on-line service provider or other organization that is responsible for arranging e-mail address for the domain associated with the submitted e-mail address. Torstar Corp. and/or D.L. Blair Inc. assumes no responsibility for any computer injury or damage related to or resulting from accessing and/or downloading any sweepstakes material. Rules are subject to any requirements/ limitations imposed by the FCC. Purchase or acceptance of a product offer does not improve your chances of winning.

For winner's name (available after May 1, 2002), send a self-addressed, stamped envelope to: Harlequin Mother's Day Contest Winners 2216, P.O. Box 4200 Blair, NE 68009-4200 or you may access the www.eHarlequin.com Web site through June 3, 2002.

Contest sponsored by Torstar Corp., P.O. Box 9042, Buffalo, NY 14269-9042.

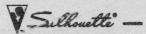

Silhouette® —

where love comes alive—online...

eHARLEQUIN.com

your romantic magazine

Indulgences

♥ Monthly guides to indulging yourself, such as:
  ★ Tub Time: A guide for bathing beauties
  ★ Magic Massages: A treat for tired feet

Horoscopes

♥ Find your daily Passionscope, weekly Lovescopes and Erotiscopes

♥ Try our compatibility game

Romantic Movies

♥ Read all the latest romantic movie reviews

Royal Romance

♥ Get the latest scoop on your favorite royal romances

Romantic Travel

♥ For the most romantic destinations, hotels and travel activities

All this and more available at
www.eHarlequin.com

SINTE1R2

Silhouette Romance introduces tales of enchanted love and things beyond explanation in the new series

Soulmates

Couples destined for each other are brought together by the powerful magic of love....

A precious gift brings

A HUSBAND IN HER EYES

by Karen Rose Smith (on sale March 2002)

Dreams come true in

CASSIE'S COWBOY

by Diane Pershing (on sale April 2002)

A legacy of love arrives

BECAUSE OF THE RING

by Stella Bagwell (on sale May 2002)

Available at your favorite retail outlet.

Where love comes alive™